JOHN BARRINGTON was a hill shepherd, who lived in Rob Roy MacGregor's old house, in the heart of the Scottish Highlands, for almost 30 years. With his faithful companions, Barrington gave sheepdog demonstrations throughout the summer and kept active over the long winter as a rugby referee. A noted sheep judge, he was delighted to be invited to officiate at the 1994 Royal Highland Show in Edinburgh and regularly judged in Europe.

Like most shepherds, Barrington is a natural storyteller, a gift he exercises at schools, clubs and societies, and as an after dinner speaker. Stories are recounted on the move during the daytime guided tours, twilight ghost walks, and as a commentator at a dozen or so Highland Games each year. Stories told to enliven his whisky tasting sessions are always presented in the right spirit!

Out of the Mists is his third book with Luath Press. He has also written *Red Sky at Night*, a UK Bestseller and winner of a Scottish Arts Council Book Award, and *Loch Lomond and the Trossachs*.

D1393257

Out of the Mists

JOHN BARRINGTON

Luath Press Limited

EDINBURGH

www.luath.co.uk

First published 2008

ISBN (10): 1-905222-33-5
ISBN (13): 978-1-905222-33-9

The publishers acknowledge the support of

 Scottish
Arts Council

towards the publication of this volume.

The paper used in this book is recyclable. It is made from
low chlorine pulps produced in a low energy, low emission manner
from renewable forests.

Printed and bound by
Bell & Bain Ltd., Glasgow

Typeset in 10.5 point Sabon
by 3btype.com

*To all the storytellers who have brought
these tales out of the mists of time.*

Contents

Foreword by Donald Smith   9
Preface   11

ANIMALS
Introduction   13
1   The Story of Bran   13
2   Battle of the Bulls   16
3   The Grey Two-Horned Sheep   20
4   The Last Dragon in Stirling   24
5   Noah and the Unicorns   28

FAERIES
Introduction   32
6   Oak Royal   33
7   The Ball of Gold   36
8   Ben Ime   39
9   Disobedient Donald   43
10 The Faerie Queen's Ball   47

GHOSTS
Introduction   50
11 Out of the Mists   50
12 Donald of the Wailing Drones   54
13 Ellen's Isle   57
14 Visitors to Iona   61
15 Robert Kirk   64

GIANTS
Introduction   68
16 Gog and Magog   68
17 Arthur   72

18 Three Golden Hairs   76
19 Corryvreckan   80
20 The Giant's Causeway   84

OSSIAN
Introduction   89
21 Ossian's Wife   89
22 The Stag Hunt   93
23 White Heather   96
24 Finn's Big Sleep   98
25 Ossian's Ring   101

SAINTS
Introduction   106
26 Scotland's First Patron Saint   106
27 Saint Andrew   109
28 Saint Columba   112
29 Saint Fillan   116
30 Saint Fiacre   120

SIGNIFICANT TRAVELLERS
Introduction   124
31 Jesus' Visit to Scotland   124
32 The Devil's Visit   127
33 Ebenezer Erskine   131
34 MacGregor's Potion   134
35 Cesare   137

WITCHES
Introduction   141
36 Good Witches   141
37 Bad Witch   144
38 The Wickedest Witch   148
39 Travelling Witches   151
40 The Last Witch   155

Afterword   159

Foreword

Reading this book is like being invited to an extended Highland ceilidh. After a long day's travelling you arrive at a croft house and are welcomed to join the neighbours around the peat fire. This is not a ceilidh in the sense of 'country dance' but in the original sense of a neighbourly gathering, to exchange news, stories, songs, music and perhaps sometimes a step dance.

At any rate, for this storytelling ceilidh there is a very distinctive host – the man of the house. He is a dynamic presence, compact and kilted, but without bombast or self promotion. He is a reassuring presence but, as he moves into storytelling mode, you realise that he is energetic and brimming with humour. He gives himself to the story, and invites you into the world of a Scottish storyteller.

This is John Barrington. You may already have encountered John Barrington the shepherd, or John Barrington the best-selling author of *Red Sky at Night*. But this is different. Here is a storytelling artist who has immersed himself in all aspects of Highland storytelling tradition.

You will be treated to lore and legend, history and myth, religion and witchcraft, fact and fantasy, but all rolled into one seamless whole. The story is the thing. The landscapes and seasons are here, along with the history, humour and dreams of the Scottish Highlands. It is an education and an entertainment all at once.

John Barrington has his feet firmly on Scottish ground but his eye, imagination and spirit, are all alive to an ancient culture that cannot be lost as long as the voice of the storyteller is still heard in the land. Listen and enjoy.

Donald Smith, Director
The Scottish Storytelling Centre

Preface

THESE STORIES HAVE come to me through the ancient art of story-telling and will be far better by being read aloud – if only to yourself.

For the greater part of our history we have relied on storytellers passing on their tales, loaded with knowledge and information, down through countless generations. Stories were also used to explain anything that was otherwise quite inexplicable. It was the Scottish Education Act 1696 that brought a more structured learning system into place. In fact, Scotland was the first nation since the days of ancient Sparta to make education available for every child.

The most famous storyteller of all was Ossian, the third son of the great warrior chief, Finn McCoul, fourth century leader of Fianna. I have been told that the Fianna were remarkable people, standing over seven ft tall – and those were just the ladies. It seems that Finn and his people only had two interests in life – fighting and hunting. Fortunately, Ossian was able to put his father's adventures into stories that could be remembered and recounted time and time again.

In 1975 I stumbled, almost by accident, into one of the last bastions of the oral storytelling tradition. In the middle of winter, I came with my family to be a shepherd in the heart of the Trossachs. My new shepherding colleagues, and other neighbours in the glen, were soon telling me stories about the history, wildlife, folklore and legends of the area. Through these stories I was introduced to many great characters, not least Rob Roy MacGregor, in whose house we were living, and Ossian.

My earliest interest in storytelling was in the tales told to me by both of my grandfathers. Over the years I have been fortunate enough to be given wonderful stories, freely passed on by numerous other storytellers, all skilled in their craft. As a member of the Scottish Storytelling Centre, I have come to appreciate all the work being undertaken to nurture and promote storytelling throughout the land, and further afield, too. Without any of these, I simply would not have become a storyteller.

I am also indebted to all at Luath Press, Edinburgh, who had sufficient faith in me to publish this collection of stories. Luath was the favourite sheepdog of another of Scotland's great storytellers, Robert Burns.

Animals

FROM HIS EARLIEST days Man's existence has been inextricably entwined with the animals which provided companionship, food and clothing and, in many cases, a direct link to the supernatural Otherworld. Throughout history animals have been sacrificed to appease the gods. Sometimes gory entrails would be spilled for a soothsayer to see into the future and, even today, birds and animals are said to foretell the weather – and even death. It was widely believed that some animals, and certain people, had the ability to completely change shape and every witch and warlock would be attended by an animal or familiar, through which sorcery could be channelled and enhanced.

Rituals and stories of animals go right back to the time of Adam, when Eve was tempted by a serpent. Ancient cave paintings illustrated the animals upon which the people depended and the oldest stone carvings of the Celts depict bulls, sheep and dogs, as well as dragons and unicorns. As it happens, each of these sculpted stone animals feature in their own story in this first chapter, beginning with one of the tales of Ossian.

1 The Story of Bran

Undoubtedly, the most celebrated of all storytellers is Ossian, the third son of the warrior chief, Fionn Mac Cumhaill – in English, Finn MacCoul. Ossian was able to take the great adventures of his father's people, the battles the Fianna fought and the hunts that they enjoyed, and put them into story form.

Many great tales can, and will, be told about the great Finn Mac-Coul, but this one concerns one of Finn's greatest allies, Bran. 'The Story of Bran' begins with the capture of Finn by his greatest enemy, Cormac Mac Airt. The two men had been at war for many years, as Cormac's Picts and Finn's Scots had fought over territory, live-stock, women – and anything else they could think of. Finn was quickly carried off to Cormac's stronghold, not far from present day Inverness. As he was now beyond immediate rescue, it was down to negotiation for his release, usually a long and drawn out affair. Cormac was in no hurry to come to the table, not until he had carefully considered all his options. In the meantime, without their leader, the Scots would be unlikely to launch an attack.

The very first demand made by the King of the Picts was for a large number of slaves so reducing the enemy's manpower at a stroke. When this demand was relayed back to Finn's people, they readily agreed. After all, they could get them all back some day pretty soon.

Then Cormac's negotiators insisted on the handing over of enough cattle and sheep as would fill the Great Glen. Now this was a double edged demand. Not only were these animals the principal unit of currency, but meeting such an obligation would bring famine and weakness upon the Scots. However, it was agreed, and droves of sheep and cattle poured into the Great Glen. The followers of Finn MacCoul could always get their livestock back tomorrow.

At the next round of negotiations the Picts demanded vast tracts of land, reclaiming many of their lost territories. Lorne, Lochaber and the Badenoch were to be returned to Cormac Mac Airt. It was from these places that Finn could have called upon the services of many good fighting men and been furnished with plentiful supplies of corn and meat to sustain them. This, too, would be quite a loss. But for Finn to be safely returned, these lands had to be conceded. They could always get them back tomorrow.

The fourth and final demand was rather unusual. In order to secure the freedom of their leader, the Fianna would have to arrange a procession of two of every animal under the sun, to pass before King Cormac as part of his victory parade. Baffled, the negotiators returned home with this seemingly impossible mission.

Finn, whose own mother was a faerie, had been given two great hunting dogs by the Little People who were called Bran and Sgeolan *(pronounced Skilarn)*. These hounds were full brothers, although born from different litters. Bran and Sgeolan were no ordinary hounds; their mother was a woman who had been turned into a wolfhound bitch by her husband's mistress, and they had more than a few human characteristics. When Bran and his brother overheard these apparently impossible conditions being discussed, they sent the negotiating team back to the table to ask for a date. And the two dogs would arrange everything. If Finn had any chance at all of being returned alive, his fate certainly rested with his faithful hounds. Cormac, of course, had set the impossible task because he had no real intention of ever releasing his deadliest enemy.

Bran sent his brother away into the hills to find the animals. Sgeolan is often spoken about as the Old Grey Dog, an apt description for this hound, whose coat was the colour and texture of the morning mist. He travelled through the glens and over the high passes, but no human eye fell upon him. Sgeolan knew well that the life of his master depended on the success of his quest. Meantime, Bran had returned to the Underworld, to seek advice from the Faeries. They could do little in practical terms because Cormac had Finn imprisoned within an iron cage, against which faerie power was bound to fail. But counsel they could give. Bran was told many things that would help to bring Finn MacCoul back to his people.

On the appointed day, Cormac was seated on his golden throne, under a golden canopy, surrounded by many of his chiefs and pagan druids. From his vantage point on the top of the Cnoc, a rounded hill not far from Inverness, Cormac could look down on his great victory parade. First came the Pictish warriors, enjoying this moment of glory, full of high spirits and heather ale! Next came the Scots women and children, now in bondage, groaning under a burden of golden treasure. Much of which had been looted from Cormac's newly acquired territories. The slaves were followed by the Scottish prisoners of war, crawling past on their hands and knees, in complete subjugation to the Pictish King. It was now time for the grand finale.

An expectant hush fell upon the crowd. Where were the animals? The tension began to grow and nothing seemed to be happening. Suddenly, from the mist shrouded glen to the north of the Cnoc, the first of the animals emerged. The faerie hounds had very cleverly placed the two mice in front of the two cats, with the two dogs right behind! The two hares, there were no rabbits in Britain at that time, were in front of the foxes and the sheep under the noses of the wolves. The thick mist had parted, rolling along on both sides of the long line of animals as they came forward two by two. The two highland cattle were almost at the back of the parade, using their long, sharp horns to keep things moving. But right at the back came the whales.

Cormac had indeed demanded that two of every animal should be included in his parade – and whales really are animals. They may look like fish, and they do live in the sea, but whales are true, warm blooded mammals. King Cormac was so impressed by the walking of the whales that, against his better judgement, he decided to keep his word and release Finn from captivity. When Finn MacCoul was told that he owed his life to his faithful hounds, he spoke just three words – *Mo bheannachd orra*; Good on them!

2 Battle of the Bulls

Celtic people looked upon cattle as the most important and valuable gift to be bestowed on Man by the ancient gods. The provision of cattle was seen as essential to the wellbeing, if not survival, of the human race. Cows would produce milk with their calves, provide meat for the community and, ultimately, hides to be turned into leather. Until quite recent times the economy of the Scottish

Highlands was based on cows, rather than on money. If a man had no cows he would be destitute, there would be no milk to help sustain his family, and no calf to pay the rent. A single cow would find herself greatly overworked, trying to provide enough milk for her own calf and the family's needs. But things were a little better than having no cattle.

With two cows, life was a lot more comfortable all round. Careful management would ensure that one cow calved and came into milk each year, while the other cow rested and regained her strength.

A man with three cows was deemed to be well off. Surplus milk would be churned into butter and pressed into cheese, and stored up for winter consumption. His well-fed calves would quickly grow into large and valuable assets.

Four cows meant that a man was rich, and with five cows he was filthy rich! And no Highlander could ever understand anyone needing more than five cows. Trying to feed extra animals, and keep them alive through the long winter months, would be a problem in itself.

Through time, the Celtic people began to organise themselves into larger groups, mostly drawn together by family ties. This was the start of the clan system. Communal living involved the pooling of resources, principally manpower, and sharing the benefits of increased production – more food. The cattle, too, were gathered into larger herds, known in the Highlands as folds. It is impossible to overstate the value of these animals as they represented the entire bankroll of a community. Not only were these cattle subjected to the usual problems of food shortages and disease, they could also be stolen. The practice of reiving and redistributing cattle became widespread, almost a national sport, with strict rules of conduct.

The first rule was not to have your livestock lifted, spirited away from under your noses. This was the responsibility of a herdsman who knew every individual animal in his care. His duties were to keep his charges well away from any growing crops, prevent them wandering towards dangerous places – and to look out for raiders. This was called warding, from Old English, *weard* and Old Norman French, *warde* – to keep safe. The beasts would be protected from the severe highland weather by long, shaggy coats and most would be black, the colour of native Celtic cattle. Hence the expression, blackmail, originally any payment (Gaelic, *mal*) made with black cattle. Now it means a payment made under a degree of duress!

The red cattle, which we know today as Highland cows, were introduced by the Vikings, along with people with blond hair and a penchant for burning, pillaging and raping – the enduring Folk Memory of the Scots has retained a strong dislike of being visited by fair headed men, particularly at Hogmanay. White cattle had been brought to these shores by the Romans. They were big, they were beautiful and gave lots of milk. They were also extremely soft and the Scottish climate did not suit them, at all. In an age where a man's wealth was counted, not in gold or silver coin, but in his livestock, to own a rare white bull would set you apart from your peers. Holding on to your white bull would be the difficult part.

Long ago, the MacGregors of Glengyle were the proud owners of a magnificent white bull. Their territory ran from the north-east corner of Loch Lomond to the Trossachs, a distance of about 15 miles. In the other direction, northwards from the shores of Loch Katrine, Clan Gregor covered no more than five miles. Within this area there were many townships and settlements, each with their own folds of cattle. This was the range of the white MacGregor bull. One of the chief's finest men would accompany the animal wherever it roamed, acting as warder to the 'Pride of the clan'. The more cows this great bull could cover, the better the chances of white offspring, particularly very valuable young white bulls.

On the west side of Loch Lomond lay the vast, mountainous

lands of the MacFarlane's. Here, too, wandered a mighty stock bull, every bit as big and powerful as Clan Gregor's, but red in colour. On occasion the two bulls would eye each other up, bellowing challenges across the deep water. The neighbouring clans got on quite well with one another, facing mutual dangers side by side. Their bulls, however, exuded such mutual animosity that, at times, the clansmen had the utmost difficulty keeping them apart. One dark night the white bull slipped away from his minder and made off under a cloak of complete blackness. By the time he was missed, the white bull was miles away, half way up Loch Lomondside.

As the first light came into the morning sky, the MacGregor bull found himself deep inside his adversary's territory. In spite of the best efforts of MacFarlane's men, the red bull would not be denied. He was more than prepared to engage in mortal combat. The two enormous animals collided at full speed, locking horns high on the hillside above Stuckendroin Farm. Fur flew and the earth trembled! The battle was so violent that an entire mountain was demolished, trampled down to form the Little Hills now standing in its place. A great mass of rocks and boulders crashed down to the lochside, almost completely cutting off the north from the rest of the west shore. To this day there is only a single track road picking its way through the debris.

Finally, the broken body of the red bull tumbled down the mountain and landed deep in a bog. The victor contemptuously tossed a huge boulder, landing the distinctive stone on top of his vanquished foe, and returned home. The massive grave marker became known as *Clach nan tarbh*, 'Stone of the Bull'. Later it became the Pulpit Rock, first used for secret services by the persecuted Covenanters. In 1825 worship at the rock was resumed. A vestibule was blasted out, to provide shelter for the minister and precentor, who led the singing. It was another 70 years before a church was built.

For many months after his victory the white bull of Clan Gregor became a very red bull, until the rains washed out the bloodstains from his coat. The influence of that great animal can still be seen today. Every year, on Midsummer's Day, as part of their annual land rent, a white bull calf must be paid by the MacIntyres of Lorne to Clan Campbell. Each and every one of those young bulls could trace his lineage back to the Great White Bull of Glengyle.

3   The Grey Two-Horned Sheep

Long ago, at a time when Scotland was divided up into many smaller countries, there was a King who was very happy with life. He had a prosperous kingdom and a lovely wife and a beautiful daughter, both of whom had exquisite golden hair. In this time when wealth was measured in the value of your livestock, it was the Fair Princess herself who looked after her father's sheep. If cattle were used to sustain the economy, then sheep were used to sustain the community as every part of a sheep could be put to good use. There was wool to spin and woven into cloth, meat to eat, fat for candles and milk to be turned into cheese. Even the droppings were used to manure the land. Finally, there were the bare bones for burning. A sheep's bone gives out more heat than a lump of coal of the same size. The bone ash, burned with wood and peat, was also used as a fertiliser, greatly enriching the soil.

The native sheep were small, dark woolled and extremely hardy. They also had four horns and short tails, quite different from the sheep we see today. It was the Romans who introduced much larger sheep, with white wool, long tails and only two horns on their heads. Roman sheep also had very pronounced roman noses. British farmers were very quick to start crossing these white Roman sheep onto the native breeds, producing larger animals and much better wool. Unfortunately, the new sheep did not think much of the local Scottish climate and it was only the most skilful shepherds who could prevent them dying off in large numbers. The Fair Princess had one of these sheep in her flock, in fact, it was her favourite animal. This was a ewe with a lovely pale grey fleece and, after the Roman fashion, only two horns.

Then, quite unexpectedly, the Queen took ill and died. Everybody was very sad and the entire country went into mourning. After a long time the people began to cheer up and, when the King married again, the whole population rejoiced. The new Queen had been a widow, with a daughter of her own. Both were raven haired and, while the mother was pretty, the new princess was as ugly as sin. The two princesses were exactly the same age but quite different in character, one bright and sunny and the other sullen and dark, just like her hair. The Dark Princess was spiteful, too. She would wrongfully accuse her stepsister of terrible things, often having done them herself. As punishment, the Queen would send the Fair Princess to tend her sheep with no food for the whole long day, day after day after day. And she would be given nothing to eat at home, either.

Even though the Fair Princess was being starved, she remained as cheerful as always and the bloom never left her cheeks. The cruel stepmother became suspicious of her good graces. Knowing something very strange was going on she sent her own daughter to spy on her stepsister, telling her to watch every move the Fair Princess made. It was like having a second shadow. The Dark Princess didn't like sheep but followed the shepherdess around the hillsides as she tended her flock. At noon the pair stopped to rest, sitting on the soft grass, the dark one eating a fine luncheon, the fair lass going hungry. A pair of sea eagles soared high overhead as the dark coated sheep grazed round about them. When the food had been finished, eaten to the last crumb, the Fair Princess offered to comb her stepsister's hair.

With the warm sun on her skin and the gentle grooming of her hair, the well fed girl soon fell fast asleep. At this point, the grey, two-horned sheep came quietly forward, almost as though she was on tip-toes. While her stepsister slumbered, the Fair Princess was able to draw rich, nutritious milk from the ewe, into her own hand, and feed herself. So this was the secret of her survival. Unfortunately, the Dark Princess had several large scabs on her scalp, well hidden by dull, thick, black hair. And under each of these festering scabs was an eye that never slept. The secret was soon told to the Queen who immediately arranged a great banquet, at which the main course to be served would be the grey sheep with the two horns.

Now it so happened that a Prince in a far away land had been told of a beautiful Princess whose hair outshone the sunshine. He knew she would be found tending her father's flock, where the sheep grew the finest wool and produced the sweetest meat. So off he went, on a quest to find his future wife. The Prince searched through many countries but their sheep all looked like any other sheep. He eventually came to one distant land where the sheep were as poor, dull and scabby as the ugly shepherdess and, without a second glance, he travelled on. The sad sheep were missing the loving care of the Fair Princess, now imprisoned at the castle, always under the eye of her wicked stepmother. After much fruitless searching, the Prince returned home and consulted a Wise Woman. She told the Prince to retrace his path from last to first, taking with him a pair of slippers that would only properly fit one girl; they were beautiful, precious slippers of glass.

When the Queen heard that a handsome Prince would soon be knocking at the door, looking for his bride-to-be, she began to lay her cunning plans for the Prince to marry her own daughter, no less. First of all the Queen sent her husband to a far away place, to hunt a certain wild goose. Then she had the Fair Princess chained to the wall of a cave, hidden in the rocks below the raven's eyrie. By this time the poor girl had become extremely thin and wan.

The Prince arrived, the King and his daughter were both well out of sight, but there was still a problem – getting her own daughter's big feet into the rather dainty glass slippers. There was only one thing for it – cut them down to size! After much sawing and hacking and a great deal of bandaging, the Dark Princess was presented to the Prince and, of course, the glass slippers fitted perfectly.

As if by magic, a wedding feast appeared and then a priest appeared too. The Queen announced the wedding would take place at once. The poor Prince was simply dumbfounded about the choice of his wife but he knew that these slippers were made from the rarest and most magical material and could never be untrue. This ugly creature must become his bride. Suddenly a raven appeared, flying around the great hall and telling everyone to look for the blood! Blood? Where could this blood be? Then the Prince noticed the blood, oozing through the Dark Princess's bandages and slowly filling each glass slipper. The slippers really could not lie, after all.

The story, of course, has a happy ending. The Fair Princess was soon rescued, the King was called back from his wild goose chase and the young couple were married by the priest. At the great wedding feast, the last of the grey, two-horned sheep was eaten and the last of her bones picked clean.

Before retiring on her wedding night, the fairest of brides placed all the bones she had carefully collected, the bones of her favourite sheep, and wrapped them inside the pale, grey woolled skin. The Fair Princess then carried her soft bundle out into the night, and left it on the hillside. Before the first light had come into the morning sky, the grey, two-horned ewe was grazing over her usual pasture – fully restored to life! Unfortunately, a few of the tiny foot bones, belonging to the grey sheep with two horns, were either boiled away in the soup-pot or thrown to the dogs. They were missing. So, for ever after, the grey, two-horned ewe was a touch lame, but not nearly as lame as the Dark Princess!

4 The Last Dragon of Stirling

Long ago Stirling was the capital of Scotland, surrounded on all sides by a great morass that kept the town safe from attack. From his lofty battlements King James could see the one and only road, coming from the south towards Stirling. At that time the road, running through the town and north to the distant Highlands, provided the only link between the two halves of his kingdom. Stirling has been described as the bejewelled brooch clasped at the throat of Scotland, and it was said that whoever held her castle possessed the keys to the nation. The town was a prosperous place. Farmers came from miles around to sell their produce and merchants brought goods from far and wide. Amongst all this hustle and bustle, nobody noticed the dragon.

This was just a baby dragon, not long having left his mother's care to make his own way in the big, wide world. The young dragon made his lair in a small but comfortable cave in the Campsie Fells, a range of low hills to the west of Stirling. Almost 400 million years ago, great volcanic activity tore open the earth's crust between Stirling and Glasgow. Fire and molten lava, from the very centre of the world, poured out through this enormous rent, cooling and solidifying into a distinctive high ridge, clearly visible today. This would be the perfect place for a fire breathing dragon to live, not that our baby dragon was breathing fire, not just yet anyway. To begin with, the youngster was quite happy feeding on mice and voles and other small animals and nobody minded that at all.

Very soon, when the dragon was a little bit bigger, he started to snack on slightly larger victims, like cats and dogs – and sheep. And some people began to mind about that In no time, so it seemed, the young dragon had grown to such a size that it was able to kill and eat a whole horse, or even a cow, horns and all. Nobody was happy about that. But it got even worse. The dragon, now fully grown and able to breath fire, took to roaming about the countryside and picking off the odd human being.

This was very scary stuff. The people of Stirling became too afraid to leave the safety of their walled town and nobody ever came to visit. No farmers were brave enough to bring food from the countryside. No merchants would venture to Stirling to sell their goods.

Not only did the population of Stirling become very hungry, as the food supplies rapidly ran out, but there was a shortage of other essential goods – like fuel and paper. Desperate for help the King offered a fine reward to anyone who could rid the kingdom of this terrible creature, ten of the best black cattle from his own royal herd – quite a prize. Runners were dispatched with the news to every corner of the land. Many men came to Stirling to seek their fortune, some unquestionably brave, others simply foolhardy. Off they went, one after another, never to be seen again. The dragon was really enjoying this. No longer did he have to go out and hunt for his food, his ready made meals were coming to him!

The King, in desperation, went to consult one of the Wise Women. He needed all the help he could get. The Wise Woman told the King that a man would come to Stirling from the north, bringing with him six companions. But the King would need to be patient, the time was not yet. In the meantime, the situation within the town was getting steadily worse. A watch was set to scour the distant mountains but, day after day, nothing stirred. The King began to send his best fighting men, to seek out and slay the beast. Some of these warriors had come from the south, others from the east, and a few from the west. All of these soldiers were fit, trained, heavily armed and doomed. Not one of them had come from the north.

However, early one morning, just as it was getting light, there was great excitement from the lookouts high up on the battlements. Something stirred on the road coming in from the north.

Gradually, they began to make out six shaggy black cattle, being driven by what looked like a young boy, making slow progress towards Stirling. It soon became apparent that these cows were very poor specimens, even thinner than the burghers of the town. Any thoughts of a grand beef barbecue quickly disappeared. Eventually the lean cattle made it to the foot of Stirling Rock, dropping their heads to feed hungrily on the sweet grass growing below the castle. The young highland drover was taken before the King, introducing himself as Alasdair Fraser.

The sole mission of this boy, no more than 12 years old, was to come to Stirling and kill the dragon, as the Fraser Clan were renowned for hunting dragons. King James could hardly believe his ears, but the Wise Woman had foretold that it would be from the north that help would come so orders were issued that Alasdair Fraser was to be given every possible assistance. All offers of armour and weapons were quickly turned down, the only thing that this boy required was wood and lots of it. Over the next few weeks, helped by the people of Stirling, Alasdair built a causeway, a timber road across the soft, swampy ground, stretching from the foot of the castle, westward towards the dragon's den. It seemed to go unnoticed that some of the long supporting stakes, under the causeway, had been put in upside down.

By the time that the long wooden road had reached dry land, there was hardly any timber of any kind left in the town. All the trees had been felled and many buildings stripped of their roofs. On top of everything else, now there was no firewood to be had. The people were not only hungry but cold. Early next morning, before it was properly light, Alasdair collected up his six cows, now a little fatter than when they had arrived and set off across the wooden track. He was armed exactly as he had come, with a stout stick and a sgian, his trusty knife. On reaching solid ground, Alasdair began to drive the cattle towards the Campsie Fells – and the lair of the dragon.

As the dragon awoke from a long and well nourished slumber, his thoughts turned to breakfast. Looking out from the den, he could not believe his eyes, breakfast was coming to him – six black cows and a small boy, quite a feast! On catching sight of the fiercesome creature charging towards him, breathing fire and flapping its wings, Alasdair turned his little herd and headed back to the castle. Not ready to give up his meal easily the dragon chased after them. Although dragons can not fly, flapping their wings helped them to run very fast indeed. Alasdair and his cows would soon be overtaken. As one of the animals began to tire and slow down, the boy took out his knife and killed her quite cleanly, leaving her body for the dragon to devour.

In only a few moments the dragon was again in pursuit and gaining. The next cow was dispatched, and the next, until, by the time Alasdair arrived back at the causeway, only one cow was left. The spectators watching from the town walls were sure that all was lost; Alasdair and the last cow would soon be no more. Having slaughtered the final animal, Alasdair ran for his life. Although the beast was now a little slower, having just eaten six cows, the lad could soon feel its hot breath on the back of his neck. But the dragon was also heavier, and the wooden track began to sink into the bog. Then the supporting stakes, put in with their pointed ends up, began to protrude through the submerging timbers. In no time at all, the dragon was impaled, held fast, quite unable to get free. The terrible monster was doomed.

Alasdair Fraser returned home with 10 prime young cows from the King's own fold. He had certainly enhanced his clan's reputation as great dragon slayers. The head of the last dragon of Stirling was displayed from the castle walls, a sign that the town was once again a safe place to visit.

The Frasers were credited with slaying the last dragon in Scotland, on the shore of Loch Ness.

5 Noah and the Unicorns

In the days before now, the world was full of wicked people. There were children with no respect for their elders, and elders with no respect for anything at all. Laws were constantly broken and rules changed, everybody went around simply pleasing themselves. God had been good to his people. After all, he had made them in his own image and he gave them a world that was warmed by the sun and watered by gentle rains. Although God loved his people, they did not care about Him. Many worshiped false gods made from gold, others just didn't believe in God at all. However, there was one good man on earth and his name was Noah. God asked Noah to go to the people and tell them to change their wicked ways, because he was getting very angry.

Noah spoke to the whole population, but it made not one bit of difference. Then God told Noah to build a great big boat, called an ark. It was to be 300 cubits long, 50 cubits wide and 50 cubits high, which is pretty big! When the ark was finished, Noah was to fill it with animals and take them and his own family to safety. God was going to send a great flood and drown the rest of the world. Once they had worked out what a cubit was, about 18 inches or 46 cm, the length of a man's hand and forearm, Noah and his sons could get to work. Many tall cypress trees had to be chopped down and sawn up into long planks. It was quite a long time before the ark began to take shape while Noah's neighbours wondered what he was building.

At first the people thought Noah was building a new house. When they realised that it was a boat, how they laughed. They thought that Noah had gone stark staring bonkers. Noah had built the boat miles and miles from the sea and not even close to a river. Yes it was agreed that Noah and his whole family were simply mad.

After several years of sawing and hammering, the ark was three stories high, there was a big door on the outside and windows all round. On the deck stood a long cabin, where Noah's family would soon be living. It was a very fine ark, indeed. The only thing missing was water: the ark was high and dry. But, the rain clouds were already gathering and as Noah and his family began to take lots of food into the ark it began to rain.

Now it was time to load the animals, God wanted a male and female of every kind to be saved from the flood. Noah sent the dogs of his flocks to bring home the sheep and goats, camels and oxen, from their grazing pastures. He sent the unicorns out to gather up the wild animals from the mountains and forest. All the time the rain just kept on raining. Noah put two of each of his best farm animals into the ark, not forgetting his two favourite cats. They were all pleased to get in out of the rain. Next came the wild animals, entering the ark two by two. The unicorns were working very hard, bringing animals to the ark and searching for those that were still missing. By this time all the rivers had burst their banks and made vast lakes flowing across dry land.

The ark was nearly full when God opened up the heavens and the downpour became a deluge. Water cascaded off the mountains in great torrents. Soon the ark was completely surrounded by water, getting deeper by the minute. In a few hours Noah would have to close the doors against the rising flood. Meanwhile, the unicorns were all outside, searching far and wide and hunting high and low, in a desperate attempt to find every last creature. By the time that the stragglers had been rounded up, it was too late. Noah's Ark had floated away with two of each animal, except the unicorn. They had been so busy saving other animals that they had forgotten to save themselves

Still the unicorns would not give up. They would save all these stranded creatures if they could. The unicorns organised the marooned animals into groups, herding them off to find safety on higher ground. Some went to the mountains of Africa, but they were not high enough: The tops were soon covered by the rising water and all the animals drowned.

Others were taken by unicorns to the higher mountains of Asia, but these, too, were quickly swallowed up by the flood. Even the very top of Mount Everest disappeared under water. The rest of the animals headed for Europe, desperately looking for a last refuge. It rained for 40 days and 40 nights. Even when the rain finally stopped, the floodwater kept on rising and rising and rising.

Now, it so happened that the highest mountains at that time were to be found in Scotland. Over 400 million years ago two great continents had collided and the plate with England on it crunched into Scotland. This caused the earth's crust to buckle upwards, forming the biggest mountains the world had ever seen. The few remaining animals crowded onto the very last bit of land, and that was getting smaller by the minute. One by one the animals were being washed away, until only a handful were left. Amongst them was an old druid and, as the flood covered the last summit, he used his powerful magic to grow a big scots pine tree – in an instant. But the druid was too old and stiff to climb into the safety the tall fir, so he transformed himself into a young girl, which is easy if you are a druid.

Without any bother at all, in his new form, the druid shinned up into the branches, finding herself in the company of a Scottish wild cat, a capercaillie and a golden eagle. But the water was still getting deeper. All the other animals had to swim for it, but there was nowhere left to swim to. One after another they gave up the struggle and were washed away until only the unicorns remained alive. If they also drowned, their race would be extinct. There were no unicorns on the ark – they had missed the boat. At this point, God took pity on these beautiful and kind creatures and figured out a way to save them. First, he changed their long, thin legs into flippers, making it far easier to keep them swimming. Then he removed the coats of fine white hair that had kept them warm on land, giving them instead a thick, dark skin over a very thick layer of fat, far better for keeping them warm in the icy cold water.

One hundred and 10 days after it had stopped raining, with the water lapping around the lower branches of the great pine tree, the flood water began to recede. Gradually the land re-emerged from the depths. But by this time the unicorns were quite at home in the water and God decided just to leave them as they were and that is how they have stayed even to this day. They still use lungs to breath air, as they always did. They still have their long, pointed horn of white ivory – only now unicorns are called narwhales and live in the arctic seas.

Faeries

FAERIES CAN BE seen as beneficial little spirits, helpful and friendly towards human beings. However, they are sometimes malicious, tiny evil monsters with wicked intentions. This unwelcome behaviour often caused a degree of friction between these Little People and their mortal neighbours. Various attempts were made to solve the recurring problems. Thomas the Rhymer sent the faeries of the Borders to the seaside, to spin a strand of sand. As far as we know, they have not yet completed the task.

In Central Scotland, the Earl of Menteith was not quite as clever. The Earl set his faeries to build a causeway of stone, sand and gravel, so he could walk dry-shod to his worship, at the island church standing on the Lake of Menteith.

The people marvelled as the faeries' handiwork soon stretched away from the southern shore, heading straight towards Inchmaholme. At the same time, the monks on the island began working in the opposite direction. With the faerie causeway rapidly approaching the puny endeavours of the mortals, the Earl began to wonder what was he going to do with the faeries once the job was completed. In 1298, the abbot of Inchmaholme took matters in hand, simply by banishing all the faeries from Menteith. The displaced Little People were scattered to the secluded glens around the north and west. The Faerie Queen relocated her court to the far side of the River Forth, where the abbot's writ did not run. It is from this area, so rich in faerie folklore that I have collected the next five stories. No wonder that Aberfoyle is often referred to as The Enchanted Village.

6 Oak Royal

The history of Scotland, going right back into the mists of time, has not only been handed down through the telling of stories, but also in the names of many places. On the south side of Aberfoyle, just where the road begins its scenic route through the Trossachs, there stands a white house called Oak Royal. For many years, and for many good reasons, Aberfoyle has been known as the Enchanted Village. There are more authentic faerie stories associated with this area than anywhere else in the world. It was here that the famous American academic, W.Y. Evans-Wentz did much of his work on his D.Sc Dissertation, 'The Fairy Faith in Celtic Countries', which was presented at Oxford University in 1910.

Evans-Wentz's study included the story of the local minister, the Rev. Robert Kirk, who was abducted by the Little People because he had betrayed their confidences. Not only had Kirk produced the first Gaelic Bible, he had foolishly published a book about the faeries and their ways. Being the seventh son of his father, also a minister, Robert Kirk had been privy to their innermost secrets. To prevent the publication of a sequel, the faeries simply spirited him away. However, the American scholar seems to have missed out on a much older and even more interesting faerie story. Long ago, when the land was divided up into many small kingdoms, a local ruler seems to have fallen foul of the faeries.

In the sixth century there was a constant power struggle raging between the British Picts and Irish Scots. Almost 200 years of inter-marriage between the rival Royal Houses had only complicated the issue. Conall, the petty King who lived at Aberfoyle, had a foot in both camps, although he seems to have regarded the Pictish Brude as his overlord. Conall lived on a fortified hilltop above the River Forth. To the north and west stood the Highland massif. To the south and the east lay a great swamp. In truth it was not much of a kingdom but at least he was a King in his own right. Now, kings need to get married and produce children in order to continue the royal line. In those days royal girls were more important than their brothers. Many a Scots and Pictish king came to his throne through his mother.

Marriages were traditionally arranged to take place at midsummer. This was the time that people took their annual bath – whether they needed one or not. Conall was no exception and a union was arranged with a daughter of the Scottish kingdom of Dalriada. On Midsummer Eve, guests to the wedding began to arrive, crowding into the stockaded enclosure. Long before the sun touched the Highland horizon, well to the north of Ben Lomond, a great wedding feast was in full swing. Weeks of hunting had stocked the game larders to bursting point and, with the new harvest already ripening in the surrounding fields, they could eat all they wanted from the store houses. And, of course, there was unlimited ale and whisky.

The only men for miles around who were not at the celebrations were the sentries on the ramparts. These were unsettled times and the danger of being attacked was never far away. As the midsummer dim deepened, the sun now taking its shortest night of rest, the guards began to hear strange noises. At first it was difficult to pinpoint exactly where these sounds were coming from or, indeed, what they were. It seemed as if they were emanating from the southern slopes, where the thick forest led down to the River Forth. When the King was told that his guards had raised the alarm, Conall called his men to arms and sallied out into the night. Who or whatever had interrupted his wedding feast would pay dearly.

Had they consumed less whisky and heather ale, Conall and his warriors may have thought twice before taking such rash action. But on they raced, getting ever deeper into the dark forest, towards the sounds now quite recognisable as music and revelry. This irregular ceilidh was taking place in the heart of the woods, on a smallish hillock covered with large oak trees. This was a place that no man would ever enter, if he were sober: the sacred grove of the druids. Heedless of the danger, and emboldened with drink, Conall and his men rushed on. Suddenly they found themselves in the central clearing, where the faeries were having a real hooley. The mortal King, because by this time there was more than one king present, ordered an instant attack upon these intruders.

The men slashed with their swords, hacked with their axes and stabbed with their dirks – all to no avail. On and on went the vicious assault. Hard, well-tempered steel sliced and severed the night air, ultimately smashing unopposed into the earth. Chunks were cut out of trees and, occasionally, each other. The faeries, of course, were quite untouched. When the last of Conall's men had subsided, exhausted, to the ground, the King of the Little People came forward. He explained to the astonished Conall that he and his followers had come to this enchanted place to celebrate the marriage of his mortal colleague. Now he would take his faeries away to the Underworld and warned Conall that, within the year, he would be forced to leave his home and never return.

The next few days were lost in a haze of alcohol induced hang-overs and general debility, following that midsummer wedding feast. As to what had really happened deep in the forest, at the dead of night, no-one was able or willing to say. It was agreed that it would best be forgotten. In fact, what with the harvest to gather, followed by the salting down of fat, farmed animals and hunted carcasses, the incident quite slipped out of everyone's minds.

The winter solstice came and went. Soon it was time to start the spring work. Using a cas-chrom, an old fashioned foot-plough, a good man could turn over a whole acre of land, just under half a hectare, in a month. Then the crops had to be planted, kept free of weeds and protected from pests. The work was never ending, in a month Midsummer was approaching once again – time to take a bath!

Then, imperceptibly at first, the wind began to freshen. Over the next few days the wind swung between the points of the compass, building up its strength all the while. Leaves and small twigs were stripped from the trees and scattered across the countryside. By Midsummer Eve, the winds were tearing off branches and ripping up trees and now the people remembered the faeries. The sun set below the northern horizon and didn't return: records show a total eclipse of the sun on that midsummer morning in AD885. The storm was now uprooting the largest of trees, sucking them into the blackened sky. And what goes up certainly will come down. Conall and his people fled into the darkness in terror, as the trees began to rain down on their settlement. No palisade could protect them from such an attack. Everyone headed for the hostile Highlands, they were far safer in the territory of their enemies than staying where they were.

As the sun belatedly re-appeared, the winds began to abate. But the great storm had wrought havoc. The forest of the Forth Valley had been completely stripped bare and all the trees piled up where Conall's homesteads had stood within his fort. Gradually, over a long period of time, the mountain of twisted and broken trees decayed, slowly reclaimed by nature. A new woodland grew to replace the lost forest and only a few storytellers remembered the plight of Conall. And then, many, many years later, an acorn awoke from a long slumber. Buried deep in the heart of all that rotting timber, it sent roots down into the earth and a new tree up into the light, marking the stronghold of that ancient King – Oak Royal.

7 The Ball of Gold

Long ago, before the Highland Clearances, there were four or five small townships settled in the upper reaches of Strathard. Each of these crofting communities would have sustained between four and eight families, usually closely related, pooling their major resource – labour. As the 17th century drew to a close, a mini Ice Age settled over Scotland, even the summers were cold. Crops frequently failed and the people had to struggle to keep themselves and their animals from starving, especially their cattle who were so important as currency and to provide valuable milk. Times were hard, very hard indeed.

On one of these settlements at the head of the strath, perhaps the one still being farmed today, lived a rather special young boy. For some unknown reason this lad had been befriended by the Little People of the area. There are reputed to be more faeries living above Loch Chon (*pronounced as kon*) than anywhere else in the world. They were sent to the area by the abbot of Inchmahome, who banished the Little People from Menteith, leaving the area between Stirling and Aberfoyle a faerie-free zone. The youngster, it seemed, could visit the Underworld as often as he liked, and return with no time penalty. There are so many stories where mortals have been guests of the faeries for what they feel is a very short time and have returned to find their world has been quite changed by the long passage of time.

In his everyday life, just like everyone else, he was surrounded by abject poverty but down in the faerie realm, this human boy found himself in the midst of untold wealth. Everything, if not made out of pure gold, would be lined with gold. The furniture, fixtures, fittings, cutlery, crockery, upholstery and even the toys, were solid gold. The walls were inlaid with gold, the floor and ceiling, too. There was no obvious source of light in this underground cavern, but light there was. It seemed to reflect back and forth between all the highly burnished surfaces, growing or fading in intensity, just as the Little People desired. Playing with the magical toys of his faerie friends, he held in his hands the solution to earthly poverty. This was a laddie with his head well and truly screwed on straight. He was fully aware of the value of this metal, which shone like the November sun. He knew that the old laird, the Earl of Buchanan, was happy to take his rents in cattle, or blackmail, but that Montrose, their new landlord, was known to prefer payment in siller, the term used for silver coin. Gold would be even better as it was easier to keep safe from Highland Brigands. The boy wondered if the faeries, who had so much gold, would miss a tiny bit, something quite small. So he decided to become a thief. Not that he wanted to, you understand, but it could make all their lives a good deal better. During his next visit to the faerie world, whilst playing with the golden toys, he hid a small ball of the precious metal in his clothing. None of the Little People seemed to have noticed.

Patiently biding his time, waiting until he found himself close enough to the way out to his own world – he made a bolt for it. The faeries tried to use their powers to close off his exit, but the boy, knowing this might happen, had been too clever. On his way in he had stuck an iron poker into the ground, right at the entrance, as a safeguard against faerie magic. Fortunately, he had remembered that storytellers had always said that iron was the greatest form of protection against all kinds of magic. Pausing only to snatch up the piece of iron, he ran as fast as his legs could carry him, pursued by a lot of very angry faerie folk. What terrible things they would do to him, if only he hadn't the poker. On he ran, never slackening his pace for moment, until he was safely past the old rowan tree at the edge of the township.

Safe at last from the wrath of the faeries, he began to feel excited by the success of his quest. In one hand he held an old poker, in the other was enough wealth to save his community. Still running, he entered through the open door of his house, when something strange happened. Even many years later, he was never able to say for sure whether he slipped, stumbled or was deliberately tripped-up. Whichever it was, the breathless youngster went flying, full-length into the smoky kitchen, dropping the golden ball onto the hard-beaten earth floor. The golden ball bounced once on the compacted earth, it bounced for the second time on the earth floor, but the third time it came downwards it hit the corner of the stone hearth in the centre of the room.

As the precious ball made contact with the solid stone, the gold shattered into a million pieces of sunlight and vanished. The faeries had managed to reclaim their stolen property. Not only had this boy been deprived of his ill-gotten treasure, but he had also lost the friendship of the Little People. He never saw them again. And, although he knew well where the entrance to the Under-world lay, it was closed against him for all time. He soon came to realise that trust and friendship were far more valuable than any metal, no matter how shiny it appears.

The years went by, some more difficult than others, and the youngster grew into manhood. Even in the best of times a town-ship could only sustain a limited number of people. A few young ones would stay at home to work the land, others needed to go out and make their own way in the world. Our young man chose to go into the church. This was the time of the Episcopy. At first, he was a minister in the Scottish Episcopal Church. Later became a bishop and, finally, an archbishop. And if you cannot believe the word of an archbishop of the Scottish Episcopal Church in a matter of this kind, then whose word can you believe?

8 Ben Ime

Scotland may not have the highest mountains in the world now, but she certainly has some of the best. Mountaineers and hill climbers have divided these challenging climbs into two categories, Corbetts and Munros. Corbetts are the 221 mountains over 2,500 ft and Munros, all 284 of them, are in excess of 3,000 ft. Twelve of these summits actually reach 4,000 ft, the highest of all being Ben Nevis. But, even standing at 4,412 ft/1,344 m, the mighty Ben is only a fraction of her original height. Scotland's mountains began to grow out of the ground about 440 million years ago, as two continental land masses started to push against each other. By the time all that pushing and shoving had stopped, the mountains were over 30,000 ft high.

Even before the mountains had stopped growing, the forces of nature were already wearing them away again. Wind and rain, ice and snow, all do their part in slowly changing the landscape. The tiny bits of sand, grit and gravel are washed off the mountain-sides and eventually come to rest at the bottom of the sea. In the depths of the oceans layer after layer of rock is reformed, waiting to be forced up into a new mountain range. This whole process takes millions of years, but this is the story of a mountain that appeared in just a few hours.

At the northwest corner of Loch Lomond stands a group of fine mountains known as the Arrochar Alps, a popular gathering place for enthusiastic hill climbers. Long ago it was the strong-hold of the wild MacFarlane clan, an area into which many fat, lowland cattle would simply disappear. The people farmed the sheltered glens tucked in between the mountains, growing crops and tending their own livestock. During the summer months all the animals would be taken high up the mountains, to graze the high pasture and keep them well away from the unfenced fields. This summer herding was the responsibility of the young children. Not only did the youngsters have to prevent the animals straying, they also had to milk them.

Two young brothers, Ian and Duncan, had gone with their elder sister to their shieling. This was a small, turf roofed hut, cramped but cosy, which would be their home for many weeks to come during the summer herding. Every morning and evening the cows, sheep and goats had to be milked, the cream skimmed off to make butter and the rest of the milk turned into cheese. Of all the daily chores at the shieling, churning the cream was the most tedious. Sometimes the handle on the butter churn would have to be turned for ages and ages before the cream suddenly turned into butter. It was a job that nobody really wanted to do. Fortunately, the tasks were shared evenly and everybody took a turn at the churning. Well, usually.

When, every so often, the sister would go back home for a few days, taking down the new-made butter and cheeses and bringing back fresh supplies of food, things at the shieling changed. Big Ian would do a lot less work and little Duncan do a great deal more. In a word, Ian was a bully! Besides the milking, Duncan would have to catch and pluck wool from the sheep, carry in peats for the fire, stir the soup pot, bake the bannocks – and make sure the stock didn't stray. After he had done all that, when the animals had settled down for the night, Duncan would churn the butter. Sometimes the wee lad was so tired that he would fall asleep on the job.

One evening while Ian was outside watching the stars appear above the twilight and listening to the strange drumming of snipe, his poor brother was hard at his work inside the dark and smoky hut. Suddenly, Duncan got such a shock! Sitting on the windowsill, watching him turning the churn, was a faerie. He hadn't fallen asleep, he was not dreaming – this was real. And this was a very cross little faerie who had come to help this oppressed small boy and put his bullying brother in his place. All Duncan had to do was to repeat the words, 'Ben Narnain, Ben A'Chrois, Ben Vane, Ben Vorlich and all the Little Hills' – and the butter churn would turn all by itself. And when the cream, almost magically, changed into butter, Duncan should say the spell backwards to stop the churn going round.

Nothing could have been simpler. In fact, Duncan began to look forward to the daily chore. It was this eagerness to get to the churning that aroused a nagging suspicion in Ian's mind. There must be something fishy going on for Duncan to actually want to turn and turn the heavy churn. So, one night, as Duncan went into the hut to make the butter, Ian crept up to the outside wall. He tried to peer through a small gap in between the stones, but it was far too gloomy inside to see anything. He did, however, hear the magic spell. This was too good to be true! The very next night, Ian put his little brother to spinning wool, while he went to churn the cream.

Repeating the words he had learned from Duncan, Ian set the churn in motion. He stood back in amazement as the wooden tub went round and round, all by itself. He helped himself to a bowl of broth from the blackened pot hanging over the peat fire in the centre of the room, he put a few oatcakes to cook on a hot, flat-topped hearth-stone but still round and round rumbled the butter churn. Armed with an iron poker, Ian fought off imaginary blood-thirsty Vikings and rampaging Romans that came at him from the dark corners of the small hut, until, in a twinkling of an eye, the butter was made. At this point, Ian realised that he had a slight problem. He had no idea how to stop the churn.

He tried asking it to stop, even asking very politely but to no avail. He tried shouting at it. He tried physically holding it, but it simply turned him right over on his head and kept on churning away.

By this time the churn was filled to bursting point. In fact, butter was beginning to seep out from under the churn lid and dripping onto the ground. Soon the drips turned into a trickle and the trickle quickly became a flow. Butter covered the floor and began to fill up the hut. It smothered the peat fire and began to surge out of the door. Then the butter streamed through the tiny window, squeezed out between the stones in the walls and oozed under the turfs on the roof. A vast yellow loch spread across land and began to slide down the hillside. The animals were just settled for the night, Duncan keeping his eye on them, spinning wool on his drop-spindle, when the wave of butter bore down on them. The cows, sheep and goats all took off for home, chased by Duncan who had to stop them getting anywhere near the growing crops. The butter was Ian's problem.

Ian had escaped from the flood of butter by racing up the mountainside and was now sitting on a rock watching the yellow torrent disappearing into the gloaming. It seemed that very soon every house in every township down below would be buried in butter. Boy, was he in trouble? On the next rock, in the gathering gloom, sat a small figure. At first, Ian could not make out what it was as he had never seen one before. When he realised that it was a faerie, someone who could help sort out this terrible mess, Ian was prepared to promise anything at all for its help. After hearing a full confession of all the bad things Ian had done to his brother, and to other people, and when the faerie was certain that he had mended his ways for all time, it was time to take action.

During the short summer night, all the faeries used their wonderful powers to scrape up all that butter into a new mountain. It is the biggest mountain in the area, 3,316 ft/1,011 m – that's a lot of butter! The faeries, of course, disguised this mountain to look like all the others round about. But if you dig down deep enough, you will see why it is called Ben Ime – Butter Mountain.

9 Disobedient Donald

Now it would be true to say that little Donald was not usually disobedient. Well, no more than any other boy of his age. On this particular morning Donald had somewhat overslept, by about five hours. He had planned to get up at the crack of dawn and go off to work with his father. Donald really enjoyed the long summer holidays, especially when he could get out onto the hills and help gather the sheep. His ambition was quite straight forward, if he couldn't be a rock star when he grew up, then he would become a shepherd. Donald's father was not a shepherd, but at busy times like this it was all hands to the pumps, every available worker on the estate would be sent to help with the sheep. Even children were useful.

By the time Donald stumbled downstairs for his breakfast, only his mother was left in the house. Donald's three sisters, all older than he, were already out and about enjoying the day and his mother was busy doing what all mothers have to do, even in the school holidays. After finishing his breakfast Donald went out to find some friends to play with but he was far too late. Those not out early with the shepherds had all gone away for the day. Today, it seemed, Donald was on his own. He wandered down to the pier at the lochside and threw stones into the water. He watched the steamer glide in and tie-up. Passengers embarked and disembarked and he wondered about going for a free cruise but decided against the idea.

As the hundred year old steamer sailed away from the pier, Donald mooched through the scattered community and wandered along the loch shore. Ahead lay the full length of a glen steeped in history, wildlife, folk lore and legend, all things in which Donald had great interest and curiosity. At the head of this glen stood a prominent mountain called Ben Ducteach. (*pronounced as Doch-tee*), which means the dark or mysterious hill. Like all the children in this area, Donald had always been warned never to go onto that mountain. Supposedly, there were stories of people who, long ago, had gone onto Ben Ducteach and had disappeared without trace.

In no time at all, Donald had reached the point where the loch narrowed to meet the water gathered off the surrounding hills by the river. Speckled brown trout lurked in the depths of the estuary, sandpipers called along the river bank and skylarks trilled overhead. The summer sun shone down on the glen, picking out the iridescence on the wings of butterflies fluttering amongst the golden broome and highlighting the bright white of the blackface lambs on the hillsides.

Donald was in his element. He could imagine the old way of life, the odd skirmish between Highland clans, the smell of peat smoke and the laughter of children. It is quite sure that Donald didn't set out to go to Ben Ducteach, as he was of course not a particularly disobedient boy, but that's where he found himself.

Deep within him, Donald felt such a feeling of wellbeing, like nothing he had ever experienced before. Surely, on this of all days, no harm could befall him. Turning around, the view back down the glen and the loch beyond simply took his breath away. And the higher he went, the better it got. Then he had an awful shock. Glancing down, he couldn't help noticing that his left foot had somehow disappeared yet, amazingly, he still seemed quite able to walk. And then his left leg vanished. Now starting to panic Donald wanted to sit down on a nearby rock but didn't know if he could sit on half a bottom, because that's all he had left. He was really beginning to wish that he had never come near this place. Then his left arm and hand, right down to his fingertips, simply melted away before his own eyes. This was getting quite serious and rather frightening.

Just as he feared, it was now the turn of his right leg to quickly dissolve. Followed, almost at once, by the fading away of his right arm, hand and, with a last little wiggle, his fingers. By this time Donald was quite sure that he would never see his family and friends ever again – well, if this went on much longer, they would never see him. As his body began to become transparent, Donald was wishing that somebody, anybody, would come and rescue him but nobody knew where he was.

As Donald was wondering what it would be like to be completely invisible, a little faerie appeared. She was hovering just where his right shoulder should have been. Her name was Ivy May Perfect and she explained that Donald had walked into an ancient spell left on the mountain by a wicked witch.

The faerie reassured Donald that, by using her magic powers, she could soon reverse that evil spell. With a wave of her magic wand, Ivy May Perfect uttered the magic word used by all magicians

– abracadabra! And back came Donald's body. It was a good start and already he was feeling much better. She said abracadabra again. This brought the return of Donald's right arm – right down to his wiggly fingers. And, in no time at all, his right leg was back where it should be. Just two more waves of the wand and two more abracadabras, and Donald would be fully restored. If only it were that easy. You see, Ivy May Perfect was only a little faerie and already had used up most of her powers.

Her next abracadabra went just a little bit wrong. Instead of Donald's left arm being back in position, it was his left leg. Oh dear, that would never do. Realising that the faerie was running out of magic Donald tried to help but not too much, or who could say what might happen when mortals mess with the magic of the Little People. Together they spoke the magic word and, in a flash, the leg vanished and was replaced by an arm. Now there was only a leg to put back where it should be. By this stage Donald was getting quite excited, he was really doing some magic and then, I am afraid he rather overdid things. Instead of whispering the magic word he shouted and, instead of his leg, a big wheel appeared in its place.

It was a very fine wheel, with polished wooden spokes and a shiny metal rim. Just for a moment he thought it might be quite useful, he would be able to wheel himself about instead of having to walk. But the other children were bound to tease him and he thought he really would like his leg back, please. At the next abracadabra, Donald was very careful not to raise his voice too much. It was perfect, away went the wheel and there was his left leg. With his two legs back in position, Donald turned and ran as fast as they would carry him. He just wanted to get away from that terrible place. But there was one important thing that Donald had forgotten to do. Fortunately, he remembered in time. Turning, he raced back up the hillside to thank his little saviour: Donald always had good manners.

Then Donald ran and ran and soon Ben Ducteach was a long way behind him. By the time he got home supper was ready, his father had just come in from helping the shepherds and his bossy elder sisters were back from playing with their friends. Everyone was chatting about what they had been doing, except Donald. He didn't dare admit to being on that mountain, this adventure was just between Donald and Ivy May Perfect. But Donald had learned two valuable lessons. Always make sure that somebody knows where you are going to – and never go anywhere you shouldn't.

10 The Faerie Queen's Ball

A long time ago, the Queen of the Scottish faeries was invited to a ball in Brittany, where she was sumptuously entertained by the Queen of the French Faeries. On return to her own realm, she decided that her next ball was going to be bigger, better and certainly grander than anything they could do in France. So she sent an emissary all the way to Inverness to find the finest musicians in her kingdom, two young men who were outstanding fiddle players. Now, neither of the boys was very pleased to be invited to Faerie Land because everyone knew what kind of tricks could be played on them there, but seeing that the invitation had come from the Queen herself, they didn't dare refuse. And they took great solace in their knowledge that faeries never tell lies, they always speak the absolute truth.

The messenger had told them that they would be invited into Faerie Land for just one night where they would play until the first cock-crow, no matter how soon that would be, then they would each be given a purse full of gold and be permitted to return to their own homes. That sounded pretty fair so, on the appointed night, as it grew dark, fiddles under their arms, they set off from Inverness. Through some faerie enchantment they quickly found themselves outside the village of Aberfoyle, at the edge of the Faerie Hill. Without a qualm the two lads went deep down into the under-world, stepped up onto the golden dais, put their fiddles under their chins and played. They played like they had never played before.

In no time at all, so it seemed to them, the first cock of the morning crowed. The emissary shuffled forward and gave each of the boys a large leather purse, brim-full of shining gold coin. Then he ushered them out into the steely blackness of the early hour of that morning. With the adrenalin still pumping in their veins, and the music still throbbing in their heads, the youngsters headed for Inverness. They arrived at the outskirts of the town just as the first light came into the eastern sky, and the buildings of Inverness began to stand out in silhouette. But they had no idea to which part of the town they had arrived. The two young musicians began to walk on, expecting to quickly get their bearings. However, the further they walked, and the lighter it got, the more disconcerted they became.

Neither of the boys could see a single familiar feature or land-mark that came into view. Now they were getting quite panicky. Suddenly, into sight came a building they both instantly recog-nised – the church. This was the kirk in which they both wor-shiped every Sabbath morning and in they ran as fast as their legs would carry them. It was still very early in the morning, but the minister must have been already up to attend his duties. From the window of the manse, he saw these two disreputable shapes, two complete strangers, rushing into his church. The minister hurried into the church and found the two young men now clinging to each other in absolute terror.

'Good morning, gentlemen. Can I help you?' he inquired.

'Yes. Send for Mr Macpherson. Quick! Quick! Send for the minister!'

'But I am the minister. I am Mr Robertson, and I have been minister here for 23 years'. Proudly he pointed to the painted wooden board, hanging on the wall of the kirk, listing every minister to have served in that charge. As he did so, his eye fell on the name Macpherson, the minister to that parish over 100 years before. Mr Robertson quickly called to mind the well known story of the two young fiddle players who, long ago, left their homes to play just one night at the faerie queen's ball – and had never been seen again!

As the incredible story began to unfold, and the light in the church gradually intensified, moment by moment and minute by minute, the two men began to age visibly under the gaze of the astonished minister. At the exact moment that their story ended, the first rays of the newly risen sun slanted in through the plain glass windows of that church, and the two men, now grown horribly old, crumbled instantly to dust. Apart from their strange story, the men left behind the two fiddles and the two purses of gold.

This is as true a story as we are able to prove. Both fiddles are on display at the museum in Inverness. What happened to the two purses of gold, the story does not tell me, but I am sure that Mr Robertson would have used the money quite wisely. Perhaps that was the time that the first panes of expensive, coloured glass appeared in the windows of that particular church, in the town of Inverness.

Ghosts

A GHOST, FROM THE Old English *gäst*, is a disembodied spirit of a dead person, often haunting a particular place. The Celts believed that, at the moment of death, a soul leaves the body to return home, the place of its birth. It is incumbent to bring back the mortal remains so that the two elements can be reunited. If this is not possible, the corpse should be buried facing homeward. This helps the wandering spirit to navigate between the grave and its natural home. All earth-bound spirits, those not yet called to its final destination, will always return home to visit kith and kin at Hallowe'en.

Hallowe'en is the one night of the year when a crack appears in time, between this world and the Otherworld. All through the hours of darkness there are spirits going hither and thither, most of them quite harmless but others that will be rather evil. Brave young people of every community must go out into the night, carrying lanterns of fire, and chase away the ghosts. This is called guising. And whilst out guising, to prevent any of the spirits recognising you and coming back to get you later, it is important to hide your identity by disguising yourself.

Other ghosts haunt the very spot upon which its natural life came to an abrupt, often violent end. Such spirits will remain in the same situation until, after a long period of time, they are finally called to the next level of immortality. You will meet one of these ghosts on the north shore of Loch Katrine.

11   Out of the Mists

Fife is an ancient kingdom named after Fib, one of seven sons of Cruithne who gave their names to the seven provinces of Pictland.

Surrounded by water on all but one side, Fife is 41 miles from west to east, 21 miles from north to south, and has a coastline that is 115 miles long. The land was always windswept and bare, and the sandy beaches between rocky headlands bore the brunt of North Sea gales. To many people Fife is known as the beggar's mantle fringed with gold.

Fife is first recorded as a Scottish Earldom in AD1139, in the reign of David I. It is Shakespeare who tells us that, after the death of Macbeth, Macduff, who was Macbeth's enemy and protector of the real king, became the very first Scottish earl, the Earl of Fife, in about AD1057. Much as Macduff sought to return power to his rightful king it is still the duty of the Earl of Fife to place the crown on the head of the Scots' monarch, which is why Fife was considered so important. Fife's claim to be the centre of influence was cemented in AD1411 when the first university in Scotland was established at St Andrews, under the patronage of James I. And it was at St Andrews that Cardinal Beaton built up his enormous power base.

David Beaton was born in AD1496 and by AD1524 had risen to become the Abbot of Arbroath. Beaton restored the 12th century Ethie Castle, living there with his wife and seven children but his political ambitions were already stirring. By AD1528, David Beaton was Scotland's ambassador to the French Court. Soon after, he was appointed Lord Privy Seal. Beaton's roots in France ran deep, he had studied both civil and canon law in Paris, and in AD1537 he was ordained as bishop to a French diocese. Almost immediately, Pope Paul III elevated Beaton to a Cardinal. With the ear of a pope and two kings, Cardinal Beaton had become one of the Power Brokers of Europe.

Cardinal Beaton negotiated both marriages of James V to the House of France. The first royal bride was Magdalen, daughter of Frances I. After her early death, the Cardinal returned to France for Mary of Guise, who was to be mother of Mary Queen of Scots.

The Auld Alliance between Scotland and France was rapidly approaching its peak – the future marriage of Mary Queen of Scots to the Dauphin, the heir apparent to the French throne. From that point in history, until 1906, anyone born in Scotland was automatically a citizen of France, as well as a British subject. But dark clouds were gathering over the Auld Alliance.

Into the confused and murky world of politics came religion. Then came the untimely death of James v leaving his daughter Mary, who was only days old, as Queen. Cardinal Beaton was appointed Regent, along with the earls of Huntly, Argyle and Arran.

In Scottish terms, that could easily be seen as four regents too many for all four men had conflicting ambitions and opinions. Arran soon agreed a marriage between Mary and Edward, the Crown Prince of England and eldest son of Henry VIII. Scotland had long had the union of crowns in mind but not with England. Beaton and the other regents held out for France, this power struggle was sure to end in tears. Finding his plans thwarted, Henry VIII sent the Earl of Hertford at the head of a large army, to seize the Scottish Queen, in an invasion known as the Rough Wooing.

Cardinal Beaton, though, did not have 100 per cent support for his scheme, far from it. There was a strong, dissident voice from the rapidly growing protestant sector, who were opposed to further ties with Catholic France. In AD1546, Beaton had the protestant preacher, George Wishart, burned as a heretic, but not before Wishart had inspired John Knox with his zeal for the reformed religion. When the Protestant backlash came, led by Knox, Cardinal Beaton took refuge within the castle at St Andrews and battened down the hatches; these were troublesome and dangerous times.

The only means of communication was by mounted courier, brave men who often risked life and limb to deliver their messages. Adam Scott was one such man, he had left Edinburgh with an important communiqué, whose contents are still unknown to this day, for Cardinal Beaton who was safely ensconced at St Andrews. Crossing the Forth at the Queen's Ferry, Scott quickly made his way along the Fife coastal route, passing through the numerous tiny settlements that dotted the shore. All the while he kept his eyes peeled, looking out for danger or men who would do him harm. At Lundin Links he turned his horse inland, by which time Scott was sure he was being followed. In front lay 12 miles of desolate muirland. Behind, who could tell what dangers were closing in?

Then a great sea fog rolled in and wrapped itself all around him. Scott, now hidden from his enemies, galloped on along the hard road – until his horse threw a shoe. Having to lead his mount, those behind would soon overhaul him. Suddenly, the houses of a small hamlet loomed out of the mists, a place were he could seek refuge for the coming night. The people were kind, giving Scott food and shelter, and even re-shoeing his horse. It was a simple enough place but the fare was wholesome and hearty. The next morning he resumed his mist shrouded journey. On the out-skirts of his destination the fog, which had thwarted his foes, quickly melted away. Scott delivered his message and told the Cardinal of his escape into the mists and of the good people of a place they seemed to call Hex Leden.

Later, returning to Edinburgh in bright sunshine, the courier retraced his route. Beyond the Cameron Burn, where he expected to see the place of yesterday's lodgings, there was nothing more than a few piles of stone. Later enquiries indicated that there may have been some sort of settlement at that place – but that was a long, long time ago.

12 Donald of the Wailing Drones

Going right in time, there has been intense, and often bitter, rivalry as to which clan could claim to have the champion of all pipers. Several generations of MacCrimmon, the great piping family to the MacLeods of Skye, had held that honour against all comers. Every Highland chief would send their best pipers to be tutored at the MacCrimmon College at Borreraig, across the sea loch from Dunvegan Castle. Many pupils would come from much further afield, even from Europe. In order to graduate from the MacCrimmon College, a piper was required to memorise 100 hours of the classical music of the great pipes, known as pibroch. There wasn't even any written music: all these tunes were literally passed on from mouth to mouth.

There came a time when the MacLeans of Duart sent out a challenge to the supremacy of the MacLeod and a contest was arranged at Dunvegan. Judges were sent for, supplies set in and a large number of people gathered at the great castle, high above the waters of Loch Dunvegan. When it came to the hospitality, MacLeod surpassed himself: Neither his guests or his own clansmen would want for anything.

There were several days of general feasting and drinking, just while the final preparations were being made, and to allow the last of the spectators to arrive. At last it was the night of the contest and the great hall was full to bursting. There was eating and drinking, laughter and dancing and two sets of pipes lay on the top table.

Then came the arguments. Who would play the first tune? MacLeod decreed that it should be the challengers up first with the pipes. MacLean insisted that the honour must go to the champions. They argued. They shouted. They banged their fists on the tables. But neither side would give an inch. The more they squabbled, the more they drank. And the more they drank, the more they quarrelled. Almost forgotten, the great pipes lay silent on the top table. Now fists were being shaken and steam began to rise from hot heads, and even the odd navel. At this point, Donald MacCrimmon, one of the great champion's sons, decided to settle the whole thing and play the first tune. Of all the MacCrimmon pipers that ever drew breath, Donald of the Wailing Drones was by far the worst!

To save any embarrassment, the wise old MacCrimmon sent his tuneless son on an important errand – to fetch more whisky. As Donald left the great hall and went out of the castle, he could still hear the altercation. The night was black and starlit, and a little bit chilly. He hurried on down the hill towards the inn. Suddenly he noticed stars reflecting from a sheet of water, in a place where there had never been water before. And one star was getting bigger than any of the others and rolled out of the mysterious lochan and right up to his feet. Somehow, Donald couldn't seem to get his feet, or his legs, to move. He stood, frozen to the spot, as a tiny little man with a long white beard stepped out of the ball of light. Then Donald's legs gave way, altogether.

As Donald sat himself upright, the wee man seemed to glide up to him and, from somewhere, produced a silver chanter – the musical bit of the bagpipes. Without a word, he handed the instrument to Donald. The problem was that although Donald came from a long line of great pipers, even though he practised for hours and hours, he still didn't know how to control his fingers. He knew what a disgrace he was to the MacCrimmon name. He was, after all's said and done, Donald of the Wailing Drones. But the small man levitated onto Donald's shoulder and just waited. Slowly Donald lifted the chanter to his mouth, put his fingers into place – and began to play.

The music that filled the night air was more beautiful than any he had ever heard and it was coming from the chanter that he was playing. He was by no means certain that he was actually responsible, or even if he was just dreaming. It seemed that Donald could play any tune that came into his head, spot on and note perfect. This was quite unbelievable! Then the wee man from the Otherworld, held out his tiny hand. With some reluctance, Donald returned the enchanted instrument and watched as it was carried back into the ball of light. As the shining sphere rolled into the inky black water, Donald remembered his errand. Having collected a full cask of whisky from the inn in the village, he carried his heavy burden back up the hill to Dunvegan Castle.

If things had been heated when Donald left the great hall, by the time he got back the situation was aflame! Men were at each others throats and daggers were being drawn. Carefully he put down his load and elbowed his way to the top table. Nobody noticed as Donald picked up his father's great pipes and blew hot breath into the sheepskin bag. But everyone noticed when he played his first note. Stunned into silence, they all listened in astonishment as Donald of the Wailing Drones played tune after tune. Long before Donald had even thought of finishing his set, the MacLeans had conceded victory to the new MacCrimmon Champion. There was nothing else to do, except drink the fresh cask of whisky and listen to the enchanted playing of Donald MacCrimmon.

Some years later there was more excitement, as Norman, the 23rd chief of MacLeod, brought out the clan for the AD1745 uprising. His clansmen needed no urging to rally to the cause of Bonnie Prince Charlie. Imagine their dismay, therefore, on being told to put the black ribbon of the Hanoverian king onto their bonnets. But clan chiefs must always be obeyed. Off they marched to Inverness and the impending climax to all the Jacobite campaigns. The men of Skye were sent to watch a crossing point on the River Spey and look out for the rebel forces. They watched the crossing. They saw the Jacobite army safely cross the river. MacLeod's men did exactly as they were told – and nothing more! Thereafter events sped along. The Highland army was completely routed at Culloden, the fleeing survivors hunted down without mercy. Butcher Cumberland, son of George II, wrote his victory message on a playing card, the nine of diamonds – known as The Curse of Scotland.

Prince Charlie fled south with only a handful of men, along Strathnairn. They soon met up with a few of MacLeod's clansmen who had already replaced the dreaded black ribbon with a white cockade, the rosette or hat badge of the Jacobites. The Duke of Cumberland's men, eager to get their hands on Bonnie Prince Charlie, were hot on their heels. Charles Stuart made for the House of Moy, the home of one of his strongest supporters but he found only the lady of the house and a small number of retainers, including the blacksmith there. The quick thinking smith quickly organised the defence of the house and his Prince. A few men, well stocked with black powder and guns, could make an awful lot of noise and smoke. To add to the confusion MacLeod's piper began to play, bagpipes have long been recognised as instruments of war. All through the remaining hours of daylight, Donald MacCrimmon marched backwards and forwards, blowing on his father's great pipes and playing like a dozen pipers.

As darkness descended, all firing stopped and the pipes fell silent. No casualties had been reported by either side. Except that the piper seemed to be missing. When they found Donald of the Wailing Drones, it was quite clear from the coldness of his flesh and the stiffness in the joints, that the piper had been shot dead many hours before the pipes stopped playing.

13 Ellen's Isle

Scotland once prided itself that, of all the nations in the world, she alone remained unconquered. Roman, Viking, Saxon and Norman incursions had all been resisted. All this was about to change in AD1651, when Oliver Cromwell decided to add Scotland to his

Commonwealth by force. The English had never completed any of the numerous attempts to annex their northern neighbours but they vowed this time it would be different. The Scots had simply refused to recognise the republican regime led by Cromwell and declared their support for Charles II. This schism between the two countries could only mean one thing: a bloody civil war.

At the first sign of danger, warning beacons would be lit on the highest hilltops. The women and children would quickly take refuge on nearby islands and in the crannogs specially built for that purpose. They would take with them the old and infirm, anything of value, and all the boats from the shore. The men would usually make themselves scarce, disappearing into the hills but not before rushing home to do one very important task – taking the roofs off all the houses. If you left your roof standing, when the visitors arrived, they would either carry off the timber as war booty or burn it. When the danger had past, the men would return home and reassemble the roof structures.

The frame of each roof would be covered with cabers, tossed up carefully into position, to carry the weight of the roofing material – usually turf. In a busy raiding season, you could have the roof off and on your house two or three times in rapid succession. That is a lot of caber tossing.

The flame of Scotland's ancient freedom was rapidly snuffed out under the black booted heel of Cromwell's army who burned homes, stole and maimed livestock, and abused women whenever they could catch them. The occasional flickering of resistance would be brutally put down. In the aftermath of the AD1653 uprising, led by William Cunningham, 9th Earl of Glencairn, Cromwell's troops were out for revenge. The beacon had been lit on the top of Ben Lomond, whose name means Hill of Fire, and republican Roundheads were on the rampage. At the east end of Loch Katrine, the women and children were safely ensconced on Eilean Molach – the Shaggy Island – they were all MacGregors.

All the boats from that end of Scotland's 12th largest loch had been taken out to the island and secured on a small sandy beach, on the south side. This kept them out of sight from the track running along the north shore of the loch. The women, too, were quite well concealed from view, by the trees and shrubs that grew freely on that ungrazed island. Unfortunately, they were not hidden well enough. Occupying forces, fresh from having burned the MacGregor stronghold at Glengyle, were making their way eastward, towards the Trossachs. As the night gathered round about them they decided to make camp, a mile or so from the end of the loch. Directly opposite Eilean Molach – and the women!

You can imagine the excitement amongst the soldiers when they realised that there were all these women just offshore. They began to wonder what other treasures could be found on that island. Able to see the women but unable to reach them they searched the shore soon locating a couple of boats that had been left behind. Neither had been watertight in the first place and both had been sufficiently burned, putting them beyond any further use. The only way across the water was to swim, which is exactly what one of the soldiers decided to do. After all, he had been away from his wife and the comforts of home for a very long time. He reckoned that he was easily a strong enough swimmer to reach the island and try his luck with those wild, highland women.

Soon after the dusk had settled on the water, the English trooper stripped off his clothes and quietly slipped into the loch. The dark water closed around him and, trying not to make a sound, he swam to the far side of the island, the side where the boats were fastened. The long, heavy boats had been half dragged out onto the sandy strip between the rocks. Their sterns, however, were still in the water. This would provide ideal cover for our intrepid naked warrior. Stealthily he slid in between two of the boats. Concealed under a cloak of darkness, the intruder put his hand on one of the gunwales and quietly pulled himself up to have a look around. The first, and last thing, that he saw was the glint on the blade of a claymore – as it removed his head from his shoulders! That certainly cooled his ardour.

Sitting in the boat was a MacGregor woman by the name of Ellen Stewart, waiting patiently for him to come ashore. Highlanders were renowned for their highly tuned faculties, particularly their acute sense of hearing and he was easily detected. The English-man's head would have been a greatly prized trophy. By the 17th century, collecting human heads had become a stylized form of cannibalism. Though you no longer needed to eat any part of your enemy, simply taking his head home for your mantelpiece gave you all his power and strength, but the headless body was of no value to the MacGregor women and it drifted away into the night.

During the hours of darkness, the fresh southwesterly wind delivered the decapitated corpse to the north shore of Loch Katrine, not far from the English camp, where it was reclaimed by his comrades and quickly buried in a little defile on the hillside, still known as the Pass of the Stranger. His unfortunate spirit haunts the area to the present day. It may well have been responsible for spooking a young lady rider and her horse, causing them to plunge over a precipice to their doom. For many years her ghost has also walked abroad. It is no wonder, then, that written in a diary of an old local worthy was the comment, 'No man alive would willingly spend TWO nights alone at that place!'

Since that notable incident, the island has acquired an alternative name – Ellen's Isle. Sir Walter Scott collected this and many other stories during his frequent visits to this area, searching for plots, story lines and characters to put into his novels. Unfortunately, in his most famous work, 'Rob Roy', Scott takes Ellen Stewart and marries her off to his hero, calling her Helen. This has caused a great deal of confusion because Rob's wife was really called Mary, and they didn't tie the knot until 40 years later.

14 Visitors to Iona

The beautiful little Hebridean island of Iona is one of the most popular visitor destinations in Scotland. Every year countless tourists make the short crossing from Fionphort on Mull, to spend a few hours wandering in the footsteps of so many characters from history. From the landing point, and running parallel with the present road, is the ancient Road of the Dead. This can be followed to St Oran's cemetery, the oldest known Christian burial ground in Scotland. Some 60 kings have been laid to rest here, 48 kings of Scots and a dozen or so from Ireland and Norway. The chapel of St Oran was founded by Queen Margaret in AD1080 and is the oldest building on the Island. Inside the chapel lie bones of the Lords of the Isles.

Also built on Iona was a monastery, begun by St Columba when he landed from Ireland in AD563 and enlarged by the Benedictines in AD1203 who also established a nunnery. The Vikings frequently ravaged Iona and the monastery constantly had to be rebuilt. Many of the ancient Celtic stone crosses, some dating back to the ninth century, survived the Viking raids, only to be cast into the sea during the Reformation. Since the time of this sacrilege until today, monks in brown cassocks, with a hempen rope tied about the waist, have been encountered in many parts of the island – indoors and out, though no religious community has existed there for hundreds of years. Twinkling bluish lights are often reported at the time of these ghostly sightings. A favoured location of these phantoms is the Angels' Hill, almost in the centre of Iona, a place where local people will not go at night.

In spite of all those Viking visits, and thanks to continual restoration, there is a great deal of history being told in carved stone. In front of the cathedral stands the massive granite cross of St Martin, 16 ft 8 inches high – just over 5 m. The building itself is a classic cruciform structure with a low square tower. Inside are magnificent pier capitals sculpted with a variety of birds, animals and flowers. There are a number of interesting tombs, and below the east window is a stone known as St Columba's pillow.

The rest of Iona is worth exploring, too. Separated from the southwest corner of the island of Mull by a narrow strip of sea, Iona is only three miles long by one and a half miles wide. On the south end of the island is the point where Columba is said to have landed. On the west coast is a spectacular spouting cave, and in the north is Dun I, Columba's favourite hill, giving wonderful views of sand, sea and sky. The colouring found in the landscapes, the scenery, wild flowers, seashells and rather special pebbles, all add to the interest of Iona.

The history of Iona, at one time simply referred to as I, pre-dates the coming of Christianity by thousands of years as do some of the spectres that still walk abroad. It is not only the few locals who encounter these strange manifestations, but many of the ministers and laymen whose purpose on the island is to restore the ancient buildings of the abbey. John MacMillan was just such a member of the Iona Community of voluntary workers. One evening, around midsummer, John took a walk to the White Sands at the north end of Iona. This is a spot popular with artists, many of whom also belong to the community. As John strolled on, enjoying the sights and sounds of the island at dusk, he decided to pop into Mrs Ferguson's for a cup of tea.

During his six year association with Iona, John had grown very fond of the elderly lady who, although quite blind, was always ready with a pot of freshly brewed tea and a chat. Earlier he had been quite sure that he had seen smoke rising from her distant chimney, but now, to his astonishment, John could find no trace of the old lady's croft – not a sign.

He stood perplexed by this situation, as the sun dipped into the western Atlantic and the gloaming gathered around him. The timeless drumming of the snipe only added to the sense of mystery. John walked on, wondering if somehow he had passed Mrs Ferguson's house without noticing it. Then, with growing apprehension, he realised that he could not locate John Campbell's croft either. The grassy plain where the buildings ought to be was deserted. A full moon rose into the deepening sky over Mull, casting sharp shadows across the landscape. But where were these familiar landmarks? Had he stepped back in time?

The sun seemed to have been completely extinguished by the dark ocean, the only light was that of the pale moon overhead. Moonlight sparkled on the black water and reflected off the White Sands. It really was quite beautiful. And then John noticed the snow on Dun I, as if this was the middle of winter. Not only did it look cold, suddenly he felt chilled to the marrow in his bones. As John MacMillan watched, a fleet of Viking longboats appeared from behind a small island off the north of Iona, Eilean Anraidh. Their sails stretched by a northerly wind, the ships made for the shore below. Then the great square sails with their distinctive Viking emblems were lowered and fourteen sets of long oars drove the boats onto the beach. John could see everything as clear as day.

A small group of monks had hurriedly gathered close to the shore, clearly apprehensive about this visitation. Aghast, he saw the invaders fall upon and massacre the holy men, then set off south towards the abbey. But not a sound was heard, except the sighing of an icy north wind. Time had no meaning for John MacMillan; he could not tell whether minutes or hours had elapsed before the Viking horde returned. They were driving sheep, goats and cattle before them and dragging a handful of children off as captives. Behind them the sky turned to a red glow as the abbey went up in flames. Shivering with cold, John watched spellbound as the livestock, captives and other valuables were loaded aboard and the silent longboats push off from the shore, leaving the White Sands deserted.

As John MacMillan turned to retrace his steps, a flurry of snow swept across the hillside. Then the wind suddenly dropped away. Looking back, he could see the early light coming up behind the distant mountains of Ardnamurchan – and all signs of snow had completely vanished. A corncrake rasped out its morning call, hidden in the hayfield next to Mrs Ferguson's house. The house that hadn't been there a few hours ago had smoke raising from her chimney showing a gentle breeze from the southwest. All was well at the abbey, and John was left to ponder the events of that unearthly night.

An accomplished artist, John MacMillan made detailed sketches of the longboats and the distinctive emblems displayed on their sails. Consulting the appropriate authorities at the British Museum, these specific designs were identified and dated to the end of the 10th century. Further research revealed that on Christmas Eve in the year AD986 a party of marauding Danes descended on Iona, landing at the White Sands. There they slew 16 monks before plundering and burning the abbey.

15 Robert Kirk

The Rev. Robert Kirk was a learned and scholarly man. He was responsible for publishing the first bible to be printed in Gaelic. He was also the seventh son of his father, a minister in the faerie stronghold of Balquhidder, and had all the natural abilities of such a child. From a very early age Robert Kirk found himself able to see and communicate with the Little People. Over the years he learned much about the faeries' way of life, carefully recording his observations.

This interest in the Otherworld continued after the family moved to the parish of Aberfoyle where there were even more faeries to meet because as we know Aberfoyle was known as the Enchanted Village and home to the most authenticated faerie stories in the world. Kirk became a minister, following his father's footsteps to Balquhidder and then into the pulpit at Aberfoyle. Robert Kirk quickly settled into his new charge with his family and second wife. These were interesting times, indeed. Kirk would have certainly known Rob Roy MacGregor and the young Ebenezer Erskine, both pivotal characters in Scottish history. It was at this point Kirk published, *The Secret Commonwealth* his famous book about the faeries.

To give this work its full title, *Secret Commonwealth of Elves, Fauns, and Fairies, that the fairy tribes are a distinct order of created beings possessing human-like intelligence and supernormal powers, who live and move about in this world invisible to all save men and women of the second-sight.* Page by page Kirk revealed the innermost secrets of this unseen world, but he would pay for his betrayal. Little People were determined that the minister would never publish a sequel. As Kirk left his manse, in those days a single storey, dark, dank and rather smoky building in which the minister lived, to take an breath of air before bedtime, he had no idea what was in store for him. The expectant Mrs Kirk, already in her bed, awaited her husband's return but he never came back.

The minister was observed strolling along his usual path to the Doon Hill which, after a short climb, offers some good views. The adjacent hill, immediately to the south, is the Faerie Hill – home to the Queen of the Little People. Somehow, that night, the Rev. Robert Kirk was enticed or carried off to the Underworld. His parishioners searched high and low for their popular minister for many weeks, to no avail.

Nothing of much consequence happened from May to the end of August, when it was hay-making time. The sun had set in the Atlantic and the gloaming was gathering around the village but one of the local crofters was busy working into the twilight, to win as much hay as he could for the hard months ahead. Suddenly, in the gloom of his little hayfield, he realised he was not alone. Standing close by, in the deepening shadows, was his long lost minister.

Robert Kirk gave his startled neighbour a few simple instructions, with the exhortation that he should see that they were fully carried out. The minister said that the service of baptism for his unborn daughter had to be arranged for Duchray Castle, still occupied to this day and hidden amongst the trees to the west of the village. The church at that time stood on consecrated ground, onto which Kirk could no longer go. He would present himself at the baptism of his infant daughter and the Earl of Duchray should draw a knife from his stocking and throw the weapon directly at the form of the minister. The iron in the blade would undo the faerie enchantment.

Iron has long been recognised as the greatest deterrent against all forms of magic. You can protect your home from mischievous spirits by the simple expedient of nailing an iron horseshoe onto the door so that even if you accidentally leave the door wide open, shades from the Otherworld will be quite unable to get in. And when you meet a new born baby for the first time, you should give the child a coin – not a coin of wealth but a coin containing iron. Either of our copper coins is ideal, the copper is bronzed on top of steel. A Lucky Penny does not actually bring you any luck at all. It does, however, keep away the bad luck.

Time moved on and Mrs Kirk gave birth to a daughter and the baptism was arranged for Duchray Castle. You had better believe that everybody who was anybody had got themselves an invitation to that service. It was known far and wide that the minister was coming back. It was so crowded you could not have squeezed a well oiled sardine into that room. Then, in the middle of the throng, in the middle of the service, Robert Kirk began to appear. The Earl of Duchray was well apprised of his part in these proceedings, but even at 89 years old and a veteran of many wars and hard battles he was completely unnerved by the apparition standing before him. The old man froze, unable to move a single muscle. The last anybody saw of the Reverend Robert Kirk was shaking his head at the gathered congregation and slowly dissolving from view.

Robert Kirk was called back to Faerie Land, where time is quite different to our time. This disparity is best illustrated in the story of the 'Faerie Queen's Ball'. Subsequent ministers have all realised that they are just keeping Kirk's pulpit warm in the interim – one day he will return.

Even today people are still waiting for Kirk to reappear from Faerie Land. Outside the southeast corner of the roofless church is a carved stone slab with a detailed Latin inscription. Rather than stating that he died, it tells us that Robert Kirk, scholar in the native tongue, went out of this world on 14 May 1692. The slab, itself, was placed behind Kirk's church, 100 years after the event, to mark the centenary of his disappearance. The grave has, of course, been excavated and found to contain a coffin full of stones.

This is one of the best documented ghost stories of all time, it even features in the D.Sc. thesis 'The Fairy Faith in Celtic Countries' written by W.Y. Evans-Wentz and delivered at Oxford University in 1910.

Giants

LONG AGO, IN THE days before the coming of people, giants roamed all over the land. Giants often passed the time just talking amongst themselves, putting the world to right. When they could not agree they often hurled insults at each other and sometimes, to press home a particular point, boulders would be sent hurtling, too. Evidence of these giants can be seen, liberally scattered across the Scottish landscape, massive boulders, tall stones, long barrows and rounded cairns. And all around are the strange rock formations and sculpted hilltops that could only have been fashioned by an earlier race of super beings.

Jack and the Beanstalk is a story handed down from the time in which humans were living alongside giants. This was, at best, an uneasy association, often beset by danger. Giants had a particular penchant for human flesh. These brutish beings were difficult to overcome, sometimes they could be vanquished by military might, or simply outwitted by human guile – frequently assisted by a touch of magic. Of course, one of my giant stories has to be a tale told by Ossian but we begin with an account of the very last of their race.

16 Gog and Magog

Do you know where giants come from? Sometimes these details are passed on by word of mouth, other material can often be found in books. And one of the greatest reference books of all time is the Old Testament. The Book of Genesis tells us that, as man began to multiply and spread over the face of the earth, our angels and archangels realised that there were many comely and beautiful women amongst human beings. Not to put too fine a point on it, our angels and archangels did exactly the same thing to our women as the Greek gods later did. The offspring of such a union were called Nephilim. Chapter six of Genesis tells us that the Nephilim will become the heroes of old, of whom great stories will be told. The best known Nephilim were the Philistines.

Also from the Bible we learn of a sixth century BC king of the Philistines called Gog, who lived with Magog in Asia Minor – where Turkey is today. The Philistines were certainly giants, Goliath just being one of their number. The names Gog and Magog are important, because when the Romans arrived in Britain, they found our ancestors living in an uneasy truce with British giants – it is from this period the story of Jack and the Beanstalk has been handed down. The Romans were a very efficient fighting machine, and set about the British giants with impunity, killing them as fast as they could catch them. They certainly accounted for the Earl of Hell himself, the giant of Fife, but Arthur, the three-headed giant of Lothian, proved somewhat more difficult. He was eventually slain, but not by the Romans, that is another story. Soon there were only two giants left alive, and the Romans called them Gog and Magog.

Instead of killing Gog and Magog the Romans captured them, somewhere in the heart of England in a place later known as Cambridgeshire. First of all, the Romans tamed the two giants, domesticated them and finally put them to very good use. The two giants were taken to London and were used as we would use rottweilers. Up until then, the Saxons from north Germany would make frequent raids up the Thames, beat up the town and carry off loot and slaves. Now Gog and Magog became the guardians of London Town and defenders of the people. The Saxons had to go elsewhere for their fun.

Gog and Magog did a wonderful job and London prospered and became the largest and wealthiest town in the land. The two giants were still looking after London long after the last Romans had departed but even giants eventually grow old. So, in the reign of Henry II, Gog and Magog finally left London and headed north. The people of London did not forget the two giants that had protected them for so long. When the traders' guilds got together to build a great meeting hall, on the site of the largest Roman amphitheatre in Britain, they commissioned two special statues – one to Gog and one to Magog. The Guildhall was enlarged in AD1411, parts of which are still standing today, having survived the Great Fire of London.

The conflagration of AD1666 destroyed most of the Guildhall and certainly all its contents. The Guildhall was fully restored and, in 1708, two new statues to Gog and Magog were unveiled. There they stood, side by side, until Hitler's Luftwaffe bombed them in 1940. Again the Guildhall was repaired and in 1953 Sir David Evans carved new statues of the giants out of lime wood but unfortunately the wood available was a bit on the short side and the new Gog and Magog are only 9 ft 3 inches tall – less than 3 m.

After leaving London the two giants made their way slowly northward, spending a few years here and a few more there looking for the ideal place to settle down for their twilight years. One or two places were very nice, almost perfect, in fact – but not quite. It wasn't until the two giants eventually arrived in bonny Strathard that they found exactly what they had been looking for. Gog and Magog soon made themselves at home in their new surroundings and set about integrating with the neighbours. One of these neighbours was Murdoch, the Duke of Albany, who had built a fortified tower on an island in Loch Ard – a final bolt-hole in time of trouble. Murdoch was regent for his cousin, James I, at that time a guest of the English. The regent was supposed to be raising the necessary ransom for the King's release, but it must have slipped his mind as he didn't seem interested in much more than protecting his tower. When Gog and Magog arrived in

Strathard they were engaged as custodians of this important retreat.

At looking after castles and the like, the giants were the best in the field. Just the two of them were better than a whole battalion of ordinary men. But while trying to ingratiate themselves into the wider community they became a bit unstuck. Although, for giants, they were quite gentle, I am afraid that both of them could only be described in Scots as haunless (awkward, blundering and ham-fisted). One disaster followed another. The harder they tried, the worse it became. The final straw came when Gog decided to help a crofting township that had fallen far behind with the ploughing. Unannounced and uninvited, he turned up late one night, took out the massive single furrow plough, and began pushing it across the hillside. Normally it would take four or more cattle beasts to pull a highland plough, sometimes assisted by a small horse or two. But without any help from man nor beast, Gog pushed the huge wooden implement with its foot of iron, backwards and forwards, all through the night.

The problem was that Gog could not tell when he was pushing the plough through soil or solid rock – it was all the same to him. By the time that the crofters were waking up their ploughing had been finished, the earth turned over for the planting of their crops. There was also a large area of ploughed bedrock, still known as Gog's Garden, on the hillside above Blairuskinbeg. The plough, unfortunately, was completely wrecked, damaged beyond all redemption. At this point the Wise Women of Strathard decided to take matters in hand. So, one afternoon, while the giants were taking a snooze in the sunshine, the witches cast a powerful spell upon them – a charm of endless sleep. And there the giants still slumber, on the south shore of Loch Ard, close to The Duke of Albany's island stronghold for which they were the guardians.

It is very, very important that nothing is allowed to disturb the repose of these giants. Turning again to that great reference book, the Bible, we can read the words of Ezekiel. The greatest prophet from the Old Testament tells us that whenever Gog and Magog awake again, a major disaster will occur. This warning has been reiterated by St John in his Book of Revelation. These admonitions are taken seriously by many local people. The giants have slept peacefully through the centuries, the unguarded keep slowly falling into ruin. The only alarm was when, a long time ago, the Devil tried to wake up Gog and Magog – but that is another story!

17   Arthur

Just mention the name Arthur, and already people are conjuring up images of medieval knights led by a warrior king. They would feast and carouse around the legendary Round Table before riding out to meet the enemy, Arthur always accompanied by his trusty sword, the invincible Excalibur. These wonderful tales of chivalry and daring deeds have been given to us by the pen of Sir Thomas Malory in his *Morte d'Arthur*. They are, of course, updated and polished versions of the earlier stories of Geoffry of Monmouth, and firmly set in the southwest of Britain. Geoffry picked up his information from France, his source being the work of Nennius, a man who lived much closer to the time of the real Arthur – the sixth century.

Long ago the Britons occupied the whole land, from north to south and east to west. Some invaders came and went, and other invaders came and stayed. The Angles, so called because their fair hair and complexion made them look a bit like angels, settled in Northumbria. Soon their kingdom stretched north into the Lothians and west to Carlisle, dividing the land of the Britons into two. These pagan people were here to stay. The Angles and their language, English, continued to expand to the south and north. The north Britons were also under enormous pressure from Norse and

Irish incursions and, quite quickly, totally lost their identity, culture and language. Eventually, the last of the true Britons were pushed far to the south and west, into Cornwall and Wales – and Brittany.

Nennius, a ninth century Welsh monk, realised that the culture and stories of his native tongue actually belonged to the whole of Britain and not just to that tiny corner of the land. Nennius knew that Arthur had been born and raised in Fife, one of four sons of King Aidan. Although his father was part Irish Gael and part native Briton, Arthur saw himself as totally British. Leading a small band of mounted warriors, Arthur was one of the first to use effective cavalry tactics against much larger enemy forces. Stories of 12 great battles have been handed down through the ages, fought by Arthur with his trusty sword. Excalibur comes from the Latin, *Caliburnus*. In Welsh, Arthur's native language, it is *Caledfwlch* – meaning hungry or voracious.

But this is not the story of that Arthur. Arthur, King of the Britons, was a brave man but he never had to face any giants. By the sixth century as we know there were only two British giants left and they were busy looking after London. The Roman invasion into Scotland, the land they called Caledonia, did not succeed in subduing the peoples of the north, but they did kill off the remaining giants. Well, all except one, the giant of the Lothians. The Romans called this giant Arthur and, even with all their military might, none of their legions could get anywhere near him. The problem was, Arthur had three heads, only one of which would sleep at any one time. So there was never an opportunity to catch this giant unawares and Arthur continued to maraud across the land, doing what giants like doing.

Arthur ate a lot of sheep and goats. He also ate cows and horses. And, occasionally, just for a treat, the giant ate a few people. Seeing that Arthur was the only giant left north of Hadrian's Wall, when ever anyone went missing they all knew whom to blame. It was one thing for the forces of Imperial Rome to tackle the giants, but the Britons of old knew a far better way – by cunning and ingenuity. Now, there were three young men, two brothers and their best friend, who lived in a place much visited by the giant. Many fat animals disappeared from the farms and quite a few people vanished, too. The giant was certainly keeping himself very well fed, while the people of Lothian began to get hungry. The boys decided to take matters into their own hands – and they would use guile.

The three young men went to consult one of the Wise Women. They learned that the giant was very partial to good music, fine cooking and convivial company. Since the Romans had killed all his giant friends, Arthur had become a very lonely giant indeed. The best way to deal with him would be to become his new friend and companion. The first of the two brothers said goodbye to his widowed mother and, taking his fine whistle, went off to find the giant. Everybody knew that the giant liked to sit on a hill known as Arthur's Seat. In the old days he would chat to his neighbour over in Fife, now he just sat and looked sadly across the water. The lad climbed right to the top of Arthur's Seat, where nobody in his right mind would go, and started to play a few tunes on his whistle.

When Arthur heard that beautiful music, he carried the boy off to his great hall inside the Pentland Hills. For many days the giant enjoyed the music, but when it came to preparing Arthur's meals it was quite a different story. This brother was a terrible cook. After burning the porridge once too often, Arthur dipped the lad into a magic cauldron, turned him to stone and put him on a shelf in the larder. In the days before freezers, that is how giants could keep food for eating later. Many weeks passed, and when his brother failed to return, the second boy took his clarsach, a small harp, to the top of Arthur's Seat. He had not been playing long when the giant came and carried him off to the Pentland Hills. Not only was the lad a wonderful musician – he was a very good cook.

Unfortunately, when it came to conversation and answering all the giant's questions about human culture and history, the young man was quite out of his depth. So he too was dipped in the magic cauldron and put on the shelf in the larder, right alongside his brother. Many weeks passed, and when the second brother failed to return, their best friend prepared to meet the giant. He played the bagpipes well enough, but there was one more thing he needed to do. He went to the blacksmith, for him to make a great club, long enough to fit underneath his own arm and be used as a crutch.

With a stone-weight of iron, 6.25 kg, the blacksmith fashioned a club, long enough to be used as a crutch. But when the lad brought the club smashing down on a nearby rock the club broke in two. A second club was made, using two stone of iron. It, too, proved to be too weak. The third forging, however, with three stone of iron, produced a club of sufficient strength – and enormous weight. With his iron club and his set of pipes, the boy set off to Arthur's Seat. He had hardly begun playing when the giant came and carried him off, too. The lad explained to the giant that he had been born with a weak leg and required a strong crutch to support his weight. If Arthur had enjoyed the music of the whistle and the clarsach well enough, he liked the sounds of the great pipes even more. And the boy could cook. And he could answer all the giant's questions about life, the people and the universe.

Arthur thought it was a pity that his new companion was lame. He never tired of hearing the pipe tunes, the food was always beautifully cooked and, because he had listened well to all the tales of the storytellers, the lad could tell him anything that he wanted to know. He even knew the whereabouts of the best and fattest cattle in the land. Little did the giant realise that the animals were being especially fattened-up on the boy's own farm, being made ready for Arthur to carry off. The lad pointed out three of the finest beasts, which were soon caught and their legs fastened together. If the giant would just kneel down and lean forward, the boy could loop one of the fine animals around each of Arthur's three necks.

The first of the cattle beasts was soon in position, and so was the second. But, as Arthur lowered his third head, our hero took hold of his heavy club and, in one mighty blow, knocked all three heads off the giant's two broad shoulders.

After the young boy had accomplished what the Roman army could not, killing Arthur the giant of Lothian, he led his friends to the giant's hall in the Pentland hills. In the larder of the giant's hall they found another cauldron, into which the petrified victims were dipped – and all fully restored to life.

18   Three Golden Hairs

Long ago, in a distant land, lived a very unhappy young prince. His father, the King, whom he loved more than anyone in the world, had been killed in a great battle. What was even worse, his mother had soon married her husband's own brother, his uncle. The new King was not very nice to his nephew, making him work hard from dawn to dusk, even on Sundays. The name of this prince was Fergus, although, with all this work to do, he didn't feel much like a prince at all. Early every morning, when most other people were still in their beds, Fergus would be hard at work in the bakery. Then he would clean out the stables before working all day in the fields. At night, long after the sun had set, he had to polish his uncle's armour – all of it.

As Fergus grew older he became very fit and strong, and learned many things that were bound to be useful to know, especially when he became king. His uncle, though, had other ideas. If he had his way, Fergus would never become king. The problem facing the King was that, by working so hard amongst the common people, Fergus had become very popular. Everybody loved him.

The wicked uncle would have to be very careful in how exactly he got rid of his nephew, the rightful heir to his throne. After much thought and a great deal of head-scratching, the King decided to send the young Prince on an impossible mission, one from which he would never return. It was a very wicked and cunning plan.

Fergus was to be sent to an even more distant place, to find a great big giant who lived there and get three golden hairs from his head. The Prince was both excited and frightened by the task that lay before him, he was, after all, going out into the great unknown. When the people heard of his quest they wanted to help. The baker gave Fergus some bread to take with him. The farmer gave him a bag of oatmeal that could be made into porridge. The blacksmith gave his prince a rod of iron, to use as a staff on his long journey – and keep away any evil spirits. And the druid gave him small pouch, to be worn around his waist, made from kelpie skin and fastened by a dragon's tooth. Inside the pouch was a tiny bottle of very powerful magic potion – to be used carefully.

The druid told Fergus to go far to the west, and there, at the foot of the mountains, he would find a village. The people of this village would help him, if he could help them. After many days of walking, when he had eaten all of the bread and most of the oatmeal, Fergus came upon the village, just as the druid had said. The Prince found the people were very sad because the big fruit tree, which stood in the centre of the village, had not produced any fruit – not a single piece. Fergus sprinkled a few small drops of the magic potion on the ground around the tree. At first nothing seemed to happen but down amongst the deep roots of the fruit tree, the power of the potion was killing all the worms and weevils put there by an evil witch.

The next morning, when the village people awoke, every branch of the tree was hung with fine fruit. Just as the druid had foretold, the grateful people gave Fergus food to take with him and showed him a secret path that would take him over the high mountains, to the village on the other side. They, too, would help him, if he could help them.

After many days of hard hillwalking, when he had eaten all of the food, except for a little oatmeal, Fergus came upon the second village. The Prince found the people were very sad because their fine spring of water was running with blood. Nobody could drink it – not a single drop. Fergus sprinkled a few drops of the magic potion into the spring, just where it came out of the ground. At once a poisoned toad, put there by an evil witch, was driven out by the power of the potion and the water ran clear and pure.

The villagers gave Fergus food for his journey and put him on the path for the ferry that he would need to cross a wide stretch of the sea to reach the giant's island. The ferryman would willingly help the young Prince, if Fergus could help him.

After many days of walking, when he had eaten all the food, except for a tiny bit of oatmeal, Fergus came to the ferry. He found the ferryman very unhappy because he could not lift his hands from the oars until someone else would take his place in the boat – for ever! The Prince did not fancy the idea of forever rowing a boat, but there was another way to help the unfortunate man. Unable to free his hands, the poor ferryman had not eaten, or been able to drink anything, for years. No wonder he looked so gaunt. Fergus poured the last of the potion into the man's mouth.

Instantly invigorated by the powerful magic potion, the ferryman soon rowed Fergus across the sea to Scarba, the home of the giant with golden locks. The Prince only needed three single hairs from the giant's head, but how to get them was the problem. When Fergus presented himself at the giant's great hall he was amazed at the sight of this giant's long golden hair that seemed to quite outshine the crown on his head. The Prince told the giant that he was just a young man out to seek his fortune in the world. He could sing, he was a good cook, and was able to tell wonderful stories and answer any questions the giant might ask, as we know these are all things that giants were particularly fond of. Fergus quickly settled into the giant's household, and learned the daily routine. Sometimes he cooked, sometimes he sang; he always made himself useful.

The Prince noticed that every evening, after supper, the giant's wife would comb her husband's hair with her hands, running her fingers through his long golden locks. Any strands that came loose were given back to the giant as the source of his massive strength was all in his hair.

Sometimes Fergus would go and help at the island smithy and took every opportunity to turn his heavy iron staff into a very large, metal comb. This he gave to the giant's wife, all the better for combing her husband's hair. Just occasionally, Fergus would find a single golden hair still in the comb. This he would carefully put into the kelpie skin bag worn around his waist. On the day he collected the third and final golden hair, Fergus cooked-up the very last of the oatmeal and, as soon as it was dark, stole away from the great hall.

The Prince fed the porridge to the ferryman and, in no time at all, he was safely back on the mainland and within a week he was home. Fergus told the King all about his great adventure, about the two villages, about the strange ferryman and about his time on the giant's island. But it wasn't until the Prince actually produced the three golden hairs from the giant's head, that his uncle believed his story. The King rushed to his stable and had the grooms saddle his fastest horse – and off he galloped. If his nephew could so easily get three hairs of purest gold, surely he would find more. Lots and lots more.

The King rode as hard as he could to the village where the fruit tree stood. He stopped only long enough to change horses, and sped off along the path that would take him over the mountains. There, at the village with the freshwater stream, the King called for another fresh mount, and rode for the ferry. The old man was still sitting in his boat when the King arrived. Dismounting from his steaming and exhausted steed, he hurled himself aboard, demanding to be taken to Scarba, the island of the giant.

The ferryman, once again weakened by hunger and thirst, struggled to push his laden boat away from the shore. Impatiently, the King shoved the old man to one side and took the oars himself, knowing nothing of the ferryman's curse. On reaching the island, the ferryman stepped out of the boat and walked off but the King, to his horror, could neither rise from his seat nor lift his hands from the oars. And, as far as we know, King Fergus's wicked uncle is still the ferryman to Scarba.

19   Corryvreckan

The Corryvreckan is a famous and spectacular whirlpool that has claimed many souls in its time. Passage through the Gulf of Corryvreckan can be a hazardous affair, depending on the state of the tide and the direction of the prevailing wind. This narrow strip of water lies between Scarba, to the north, and Jura, two islands off the west coast of Argyllshire. Here the full force of the Atlantic Ocean is often to be felt and consummate seamanship required to be able to read the winds and the tides.

Scottish place names can be taken from the land or the history of a place and sometimes, as in Corryvreckan, the name tells us an entire story. Long ago, when the whirlpool had another name and giants roamed the world, the King of the giants lived in a fine hall on the island of Scarba. This King was the father of many children but one of his daughters was renowned above all others for her beauty. Her fame spread far and wide, in fact, to all corners of the earth. Many suitors came to claim her hand in marriage. Not one of them succeeded and all perished in the attempt!

Each hopeful swain was set a simple task by the King of Scarba, whose name comes from the Old Norse word, *skarfr*, meaning cormorant. To prove his worth, every prospective husband had to anchor his galley in the centre of the whirlpool for three successive tides. At slack-water there was no problem but as the tide began to move through the narrow gulf and the wind started to freshen, things soon became a little tricky. In no time at all, the galley went to the bottom of the sea, and it was next man, please.

After a time a bold young giant came from Norway, himself a prince of that mountainous country, who answered to the name of Bhreckan (*pronounced as Vreckan*). Like all Scandinavians, Vreckan was a born sailor – it was in his blood and in every bone. When the Prince learned of his assignment, his bones told him to take the greatest of care in this enterprise. There was no time limit on this dangerous undertaking, so Vreckan returned home to seek advice. Back in his native Norway, Vreckan went on a long journey into the mountains, he needed to consult the coven of Wise Women.

Having braved the dangers of hungry wolves and enormous brown bears, Vreckan returned with clear instructions. To successfully complete his task he needed three rather special anchor cables. One was to be made from the finest wool, first spun and then plaited, then plaited and plaited again, until the cable was complete. The second was to be made from the finest horsehair, taken from the longest horse tails in Norway. First the long hair was to be spun into strands, and the strands plaited and plaited and plaited again, until the cable was finished. The final cable was to be spun and plaited from the hair of Norwegian virgins. This last cable took a long time to produce, but at long last it, too, was ready.

With his three special anchor cables safely stowed away, Vreckan set sail for Scarba. His high spirits were soon dampened, however, as the elements seemed to begin to conspire against him. First of all he lost the wind. No sooner was Vreckan out of sight of land than it just died. Absolutely becalmed, Vreckan and his crew sat in their galley and waited – and waited. After two days a thick sea fog closed in around them, cold and damp but the wind did pick up. This was the time long before compasses had been invented, so Vreckan had no idea in which direction they were being blown. After two more days, shrouded in gloom, the fog lifted just as suddenly as it had appeared. Vreckan thought that his vessel was probably somewhere north of Scotland so, to make sure, he released one of the ravens, carried in small cages for just this purpose.

Just as in Noah's day, the raven flew off in the direction of the nearest land. Having skilfully confirmed his position, Vreckan and his crew sailed on towards Scarba without further mishap. The King of Scarba made his prospective son-in-law welcome, entertaining Vreckan and his men at a great banquet in the magnificent stone-built hall. While the Norwegian prince was making his final preparations, studying the tides and keeping an eye on the weather, many of his friends and relatives arrived in their longboats and galleys. There were 50 ships in all, full of people wanting to help celebrate Vreckan's wedding day. But the great test still lay before him.

At last the day of reckoning dawned. The water across the gulf was flat and calm and there was hardly any wind to speak of. It was in these perfect conditions that Vreckan sailed his galley into the very place the whirlpool would be and laid out his three anchors. The first anchor was on the cable of wool. The second anchor was fastened to the cable of horsehair. The final anchor was held secure by the cable spun from maidens' hair. Vreckan and his men settled down and waited for the tide to turn. Crowds of onlookers watched from the shores of Scarba and north Jura. Vreckans friends and relatives looked on from their boats, but at a safe distance.

As the tide began to run, the whirlpool was stirred into life.

The water revolved slowly at first but soon began to gather pace, driven on by the freshening wind. The galley dipped into the hollow, or corrie, at the heart of the whirlpool and was almost lost from sight to the people standing on the shore. The three anchor cables stretched and groaned – but all held fast. Then, without warning, the horsehair cable parted with an almighty crack. The crew were terrified that their vessel was doomed, but Vreckan assured them that the remaining two anchors were more than capable of keeping the ship safe. The sun set and the water settled – and they all waited for the next tide.

Darkness had covered the sea and the land by the time the Norwegians felt the boat tremble. Both anchor cables tightened and creaked as the galley was sucked down. It was so black that, from ship or shore, nobody could see a thing. This time the sea raced faster and the winds blew harder – but the two anchors held fast. Then, without warning, the cable spun from finest wool broke apart with a report that echoed across the narrow gulf. The ship lurched violently, swinging around onto the one remaining cable. The crew all sure that their end had come but Vreckan had every confidence in his last anchor – secured by the cable spun from the rather special hair of Norwegian maidens.

The morning sky lightened, but the sun did not appear. Thick, grey clouds scudded overhead and rain-filled squalls swept in from the Atlantic. Even the proud raven on the Prince's flag, flapping loudly from the mast top, looked somewhat sad and bedraggled. As Vreckan's galley swung on its anchor to meet the final challenge, watched by the people on land and the Norwegian fleet standing by, the last anchor cable snapped. It seems that one of the maidens had not been a virgin. The doomed galley was drawn inexorably into the whirlpool. Every Norwegian ship hoisted sail and raced to the rescue but once caught in the maelstrom, they too, were unable to save themselves. Fifty-one boats were sucked down to the bottom of the sea.

Vreckan's faithful hunting hound fought valiantly to save his master. The great contest between sea and hound was witnessed by the people standing on high ground, the sea pulling Vreckan into the whirlpool that would soon carry his name into history, and the huge dog fighting towards the island of Jura. After an epic struggle the hound dragged his master's lifeless body ashore – and then he, too, breathed his last.

Not so long ago, a grave was discovered at the north end of Jura, containing the ancient remains of a very large man – and his dog.

20 The Giant's Causeway

For centuries people have stood on the high cliffs of north Antrim, or sailed beyond Mull to the island of Staffa, and wondered at strange rock formations. The tall, hexagonal, black basalt pillars are truly awe inspiring in their grandeur. The very sight of them has brought out the best work of writers, artists, poets and photographers, but most of all in musical composers. *The Hebrides Overture*, written in 1830, is one of the finest works of Felix Mendelssohn. His music highlights the mystical setting of Fingal's Cave as it takes the ocean deep into the structure of six-sided columns. The questions of who, how and why these pillars exist can only be answered by the few people who know the story of the Giant's Causeway.

The story begins in Ireland at a time when giants still roamed the land and the strange demonic beings, known as Fomorians, had their home under the sea. Noth, son of Fachtna, had proved himself the Champion of all Ireland. There wasn't a giant in the whole land who could out wrestle, out throw or out lift him. After a while Noth got a bit bored as nobody would come to challenge him. Then he began to hear some stories about a giant who lived across the water, in a place called Scotland. The more

Noth heard, the more certain he was that this other giant would be a suitable adversary. But there was a problem, how would he cross over the sea? There were no boats big enough to carry such a huge giant. So, Noth decided to build a bridge from Ireland to Scotland.

Noth pulled up every tree in a nearby great forest and began to build a fine wooden bridge across the sea. Day and night he worked and everything was going well; Noth would soon be in Scotland. Then, in a single night, the Fomorians whipped up the seas to a great height and completely destroyed the wooden bridge. Undaunted, Noth tore rocks and boulders from the side of a great mountain and began to construct a roadway of stone across the sea. Day and night he laboured and everything was going well; Noth would soon be in Scotland. Then, in a single night, the Fomorians whipped up the seas to an even greater height than before and washed away all the rocks and boulders. A little daunted, he sat and pondered on what to do now.

Noth consulted Cathbad, the wisest druid in Ireland, and was told to go and find trees long and tall that could be driven down into the bed of the sea. These trees needed to be as heavy and as strong as stone, able to withstand the full fury of the Fomorians. In fact, Noth had to look for trees made out of stone. Noth searched the whole of Ireland, but there were none to be found. Cathbad then told Noth to go and make the stone trees, they could be fashioned from the molten rock hidden in the very centre of the world. Noth started to dig out a deep cavern. Deeper and deeper he went. Soon he began to feel the heat, and then, as Noth smashed through a big rock with his massive hammer; molten lava flowed out at his feet.

A long stream of melted stone trickled along the floor of Noth's great cavern, and began to cool down and harden. Now, wielding a massive hammer in each of his giant sized fists, Noth set to work. The old druid had given Noth one of the greatest secrets in the universe, telling him that the strongest shape of all was a hexagon, which is the shape that bees use to build their honeycomb cells. The giant hammered and hammered for all he was worth, until he had fashioned a very long, six-sided tree trunk made of stone. Day and night he sweated and everything was going well. By day Noth carried the stone columns, six at a time, and hammered them deep down into the bed of the sea. At night he hammered away in his underground cavern. Noth would soon be in Scotland.

This time the might of the ocean and the full fury of the Fomorians could not undo Noth's handiwork. The hexagonal pillars remained upright, quite unmoved by the tempests raised against them. This solidified lava is known as basalt, and if you ever visit the Giant's causeway, you will notice that every six-sided column is different from any other – each one made individually by Noth's gigantic hands. Driving the last of the black basalt pillars firmly into the sea bed, the giant had finished the causeway across the water. How magnificent it looked, standing high, wide and well above the sea. The Giant's Causeway stretched all the way from Northern Ireland to the west coast of Scotland.

Now Noth was in Scotland, and he set out to find this other giant whose name, he had been told, was Fionn Mac Cumhaill – Finn MacCoul. He stopped and asked many people if they could tell him the whereabouts of this Scottish giant. Quite terrified, they all shook their heads and said that they had never heard of a giant with such a name. Then ran away as fast as their legs could carry them, in case Noth decided to eat them.

The problem was one of language, the actual meaning of the word 'giant'. Of course a giant is a huge person, often many times the size of a normal human being but the Celts also used the same word to describe a human with extraordinary talents. And Finn MacCoul was a very talented but regular sized man.

When the news reached Finn's ears that a great big Irish giant was coming to get him, he was somewhat alarmed. Now Finn, the leader of the legendary Fianna, was a big man, but he was not the biggest of his people. Finn was definitely brave, but he wasn't the bravest of the Fianna. Finn was a great fighter, but he was not the greatest warrior in the land. But he was, without doubt, the wisest man of all. Even so, it was Finn's wife, Banbha who came up with a plan of action. Finn was all for meeting Noth and accepting the challenge, perhaps he could find a way to outwit the giant. But Banbha's idea was much better – simple deception.

After much searching, Noth sat to rest on the top of a large mountain, Ben Lomond. He noticed the peat smoke coming through the thatch of a house, hidden away in a secluded glen at the back of the mountain. He would go and ask these people if they knew where Finn MacCoul lived. Little did Noth know that this was Finn's house. When Finn and Banbha felt the ground shaking, and knew the giant was coming, Finn did something very strange indeed. He took off all his own clothes and put on one of his wife's long white dresses – and her bonnet. Finn then climbed into a large cradle, which had been specially made to fit him, but only just.

Banbha went out to meet the giant, telling him that Finn MacCoul was her husband, but that he was just away to get a few trees, to build a new cradle for their baby. She added that he would be back in no time at all. Noth stooped and looked in through the open door. He marvelled at the size of the child, and only two weeks old. Noth was quite amazed as he watched Banbha feed the baby with, not one, but two whole pots of porridge: such an appetite for one so young. Banbha peered out, looking up Gleann Dubh to see if her husband was in anywhere in sight. But what Finn's wife did next shook Noth right down to the soles of his boots – she began to shave the stubble off the baby's chin. And him only two weeks old!

Banbha brought her visitor a pail of heather ale, a couple of loaves of bread and sliced big chunks of beef straight off the bone. She then popped the great thick bone into the baby's mouth and, in one bite, he crunched right through it. At this, Noth turned and fled, as fast as his legs could carry him. If Finn's child at only two weeks old was so large and strong he didn't want to face Finn MacCoul in combat. Finn leaped out of the cradle, snatched-up his two-handed sword and, still dressed in his wife's clothes, chased after the giant. Noth only paused long enough to grab a great lump of rock from the summit of Ben Lomond, using it to completely demolish the causeway behind himself. He wanted to be quite sure that Finn MacCoul would never be able to follow him across the sea to Ireland.

Ossian

IN THE WIDE ANTHOLOGY of Celtic stories, the term giant was used to describe anyone who could display extraordinary ability. They may well have been of superior physical stature but certainly were not the massive giants with seven league boots. Finn McCoul and the Fianna fall into this category, forming themselves into an early militia, modelled on the disciplined legions of Rome. Ossian, Finn McCoul's son, spent his unnaturally long life recounting the great adventures of his father's people. He lived long enough for St Patrick to record many of these tales, documented in a simple form of Latin. Once James Macpherson uncovered these manuscripts and published his own poetic translation, Ossian's place in the world of romantic literature was secure.

Before he was born, Ossian's mother had been changed into a deer by a druidic spell. When Ossian was born, quite unharmed, Finn gave his son the Gaelic name, meaning a fawn. This chapter is devoted entirely to Ossian, undoubtedly the greatest storyteller of all.

21 Ossian's Wife

This is the wonderful story of Ossian's wife.

It was a wild and stormy night. The north wind piled deep drifts of snow into the blackened glen. Caught in the storm and unable to find even the smallest scrap of shelter, a crow was swept on into the darkness, getting weaker by the moment. Through the blizzard she saw the light of a house, at last a place of refuge. This was the house of Finn MacCoul's first son. On seeing who was knocking on such a night, seeking sanctuary from the storm, he chased away the crow and shut the door. Driven further into the glen by the fury of the wind, the crow saw the light of a second house. This was the house of Finn's second son, where she received exactly the same reception as at the first. On and on the poor bird was hurled, now too exhausted to even fly.

Floundering over the top of a drift, the crow saw yet another light. With her last vestige of life, the crow made it to the doorway but had no strength to knock. This was the house of Ossian. It was Ossian's hound that alerted his master that there was a visitor, a fugitive from the storm. At first Ossian could see no-one, then, at his feet, he saw a bundle of black feathers half buried in the snow. Not knowing whether the crow were alive or dead, Ossian took her close to the peat fire, in the centre of the room, and dried off the sodden plumage. Gradually, the tiny spark of life that had survived the storm, was fully restored. Ossian brought his finest fleece of white wool next to the hearth, for his guest to snuggle into. And all the while, the faithful hunting hound looked on.

Taking a little oatmeal, and drawing warm milk from one of the cows tethered at the other end of the house, Ossian mixed-up a small meal of gruel. No doubt, there would have been a splash of whisky too. At bedtime, Ossian offered his guest the use of his own, in fact the only, bed in the house. The crow declined the offer of her host, preferring to sleep on the soft, white fleece, at the fireside. Outside the storm raged on, buffeting the stone building and tugging at the thatch. Inside, the fire died down and the house darkened. There was no other sound, apart from the cows contentedly chewing their cud and the snoring of the dog.

Overnight the blizzard had blown itself out. As the light of the new day began to filter into the house, finding ways in through the smallest of gaps, Ossian gently stirred. He rose-up quietly to revive the fire. In the still half-light, Ossian was startled to see, not a black crow asleep on the white fleece, but a beautiful woman. For a long time Ossian stood and stared at her pure white skin and long golden hair, until, at last, she opened her eyes and looked up. Wrapping herself in the fleece, the young woman explained that she had been put under a dreadful spell by an evil witch. It was clear that Ossian's great kindness had broken that enchantment and restored her to her proper form. And, providing that he never referred to the shape in which she had arrived at his house, she would become the best wife a man could ever wish for.

Ossian's wife was called Niamh, (*pronounced as Niav*). Niamh produced many children and fulfilled all her duties as a wife and a lot more, too. Ossian's great pride was in his hunting dogs, the likes of which could be found nowhere else in the land. The raising of any pups fell, as was the custom, to the wife and children of a family, and Niamh ensured that the litters in her care were fit, well grown and eager to learn. As soon as the young hounds were big enough and fast enough to keep up with the hunt, they would be taken from the family and begin their training. Ossian's dogs were the best in any pack and his puppies were always in great demand.

With his wife and children looking after things very well on the home front, Ossian was able to concentrate on his hunting, fighting and poetry – three fields in which he excelled. Just at the time Ossian was expecting his very best hunting bitch to produce puppies, news came of an imminent battle. The warrior prepared himself for war, quite happy to leave the care of the expectant mother to Niamh. But Ossian's final instruction was clear and explicit – the first born pup was to be kept for himself. If he had not returned by the time the litter was fully weaned off the bitch, Niamh could dispose of the rest of the pups as she pleased.

Six fine deer hound pups were born, blind and helpless, able only to wriggle and squeal, and suck milk from their mother. After 10 days their eyes opened upon a world they were soon anxious to investigate and explore. There followed two whole months of chasing, playing, fighting, feeding and sleeping. At this point the youngsters were ready to be weaned from their mother and to be prepared for an independent life. In no time at all, three of the pups had gone to new homes, but not, of course, the first born of the litter.

Then a giant from Ireland arrived and demanded the first born pup for himself. Niamh gave the giant one of the younger puppies, saying that it was the first born of the litter. The giant took the pup by its tail and, as it squealed, threw the puppy back at Ossian's wife, insisting that he would only take the first born. And if she didn't produce the first born pup, then he would tear the place apart and find it for himself. Exactly the same thing happened when Niamh offered the second puppy to the giant. As he lifted it by its tail, the poor creature wriggled and squealed. The giant was beside himself with fury. If Niamh did not instantly bring him the first born pup of the litter, he would not only destroy the whole place but wring her lovely neck, too! Terrified, Ossian's wife handed over the precious puppy.

The giant was long gone and the two remaining puppies very well grown by the time Ossian returned, triumphant from the war. As he approached the house, his faithful bitch, followed by the two pups, rushed out to greet him. Ossian, too, lifted the pups by their tails, one in each hand. They both yelped. Knowing that a first born of any litter is always silent, never making a sound, Ossian strode into his house to look for his chosen puppy and, of course, to hug his beautiful wife. On hearing of the giant's visitation, and the fact that his puppy was now far away in Ireland, Ossian quite forgot himself. In his anger, Ossian called his wife a stupid old crow. And, quicker than the blink of an eye, Niamh turned into a crow and flew out of the door.

The next day, as Ossian sat at his fireside distraught at the loss of his beloved wife because of his stupid temper, a black crow alighted on the small windowsill. The bird dropped a ring of pure gold onto the floor and told Ossian that as long as he wore that ring on his finger, he would never die. And, with that, the crow flew away. We don't know whether that particular crow was Niamh or not. What we do know is that Ossian wore that golden ring for the next 300 years – but that is another story.

22 The Stag Hunt

The stories of the great adventures of the Fianna have been passed down in the tales of Ossian. The Fianna were founded by King Fiachadh, around 300 BC, and modelled on the legions of Rome. For six centuries, three regiments of the Fianna, each of 3,000 men, defended Ireland against all invaders. Fighting, to the Fianna, was a passion – as was hunting. Quite simply, if they were not fighting, they were hunting. And if they were not hunting, they were fighting.

Finn MacCoul became leader of the Fianna towards the end of the third century AD. Of all the leaders Finn was by no means the greatest or bravest warrior, but he was, beyond any doubt as any who have heard how the outwitted the giant Noth will know, the wisest Fiann who ever drew breath. The Fates gave Finn his knowledge in a very strange way. One day, when Finn was still quite young, he came across a hermit called Finegas, living in a cave on the banks of a river. Finegas had spent many years searching the waters for one of the Salmon of Knowledge, said to live in that river. Within a few minutes Finn pulled a large salmon out of the river, by its tail, and gave it to the hermit. Neither knew that this fish was, indeed, the Salmon of Knowledge, until Finn burned himself in the cooking of it.

As soon as Finn put his scalded thumb into his mouth, to suck off the burning liquid that had splashed onto his skin, a Great Knowledge came upon him. For the rest of his days, if Finn needed to know the solution to any problem, he only had to return that thumb to his mouth. However, having such knowledge is not always a blessing, it can be a curse, too.

Through wise negotiations and clever ploys, Finn was able to avoid a great deal of unnecessary conflict and a great peace settled on the world. With no battles on the horizon, the Fianna decided to organise a stag hunt. This would be no ordinary stag hunt, this would be the greatest stag hunt the world had ever seen. Over many weeks, the best stags were drawn out of every herd in the land and gathered together in one place. No-one had ever seen such a magnificent sight. No stag had less than 10 points on its antlers, most had 12, and some even had 14. Every man prepared his long-legged, shaggy-coated deer hounds, ready for the greatest chase in the history of mankind.

On the day the hunt began, just before dawn, the stags were driven away from the rising sun. The thundering of the hooves could be heard across five provinces of Ireland. One hour later, the hounds were loosed and the chase was on. A year and a day later, the hunt arrived back at the starting point, having been right around the whole world. There weren't nearly as many stags, but the ones that remained were the fittest and the strongest and still full of running. With no word of any impending fight or battle, or even a minor disagreement, the hunt could continue. Once again the stags raced away to the west and, a year and a day later, returned once more – having been right around the world for a second time. This time there were only two great stags left: the hunt was nearly over.

Before the first of the pursuing hounds appeared, the gods, hoping to disturb the plans of the mortals, threw a cloak of early darkness over the two great stags, and hid them from view. By morning they were nowhere to be seen. Finn MacCoul sent scouts out in all directions, he was determined to find the two greatest stags of all, and finish the job in style. The Fianna searched all day, to no avail. There was not one sight of the stags to be had. As the day ended and night came on, Finn went for a walk and tried to unravel this mystery. As Finn put his thumb into his mouth and sucked, he looked up into the blackened sky above. And there, amongst the other stars, he could see the two great stags.

The gods had taken pity on these magnificent animals that outran even the swiftest hounds of the Fianna, and had put them safely out of reach. But Finn was not to be thwarted, not even by the gods themselves. He would find some way of getting up into the heavens and finishing the hunt. So, Finn went off to consult the Wise Women. He was told to go to Inchlonaig, the island of yew trees, on Loch Lomond, and there to search for a certain tree. From that particular yew Finn must fashion a longbow that only he could draw. His fletchers must make him 1,000 arrows, long and straight, from which Finn could build a stairway to Heaven.

The Wise Women also gave Finn a potion that, if mixed with burning tar, would make a flame that would never go out. As soon as all was ready, Finn took his bow of yew, the quiver with 1,000 arrows and pot of fire, and waited for darkness to come. Lying deep in the heather, Finn dipped his first arrow into the pot of fire and shot it up into the night air. The fire-arrow embedded itself in the roof of the sky above. With a clear view of the first arrow, Finn loosed his second – fixing it into the shaft of the first. In this way Finn was putting together a chain of arrows that would soon link this world to the stars. Just occasionally, one of the fire-arrows would miss its target and fly away into space, to spend eternity forever circling the earth.

The very moment that the last arrow was in place, word came of a great battle that must be fought without delay. A large force of invaders had landed on the shores of Ireland. For a moment Finn sucked on his thumb. Then, keeping the Old Grey Dog and his brother, Bran, at his side, Finn sent five of his finest hunting hounds up into the sky – just to keep track of his quarry. He would rush off, drive the enemy back into the sea, and quickly return to the celestial chase. Unfortunately, although the flame at the head of each arrow was eternal, the shafts were made out of wood.

By the time Finn returned, victorious from the fray, all that remained of his stairway to the sky above was a great big pile of burning ash.

On any clear night, as the sky darkens, if you face to the north and look up into the highest point, you will easily pick out the two great stags from amongst the stars. And, close at hand, you will see the five hounds of Finn MacCoul in perfect hunting formation, a half-circle, forever following their prey. If you look even more closely, you will see there are, in fact, six dogs in that semi-circle. Standing next to the last but one in that curved line is a puppy that got up there by hiding in his grandfather's long, shaggy coat.

23 White Heather

Before Ossian's wife, Niamh, left him she bore him many children. One of Ossian's daughters was a very beautiful young woman called Malvena. She was as tall and elegant as her mother had been in her human form, with the same pale skin and long blonde hair. The resemblance to Niamh was so striking that it had brought some degree of solace to Ossian since his wife had flown away.

Malvena was betrothed to Osgar, a local warlord who had been killed in battle. We can be pretty certain that Osgar's last battle was being fought in late August or early September. When his comrades found his body lying cold and stiff upon the heath, in his death throes, Osgar had pulled out a clump of purple heather. Knowing that these flowers, clutched so tightly in Osgar's fist, must surely be a farewell gift for his beloved Malvena his comrades prised the purple posy from Osgar's stiff fingers, gave it to a runner and sent him back to Scotland.

Well, the runner ran all day and he ran all night, and he ran all the next day, too. And on and on he ran until he got back to Scotland. On he ran again, until he found Malvena. The runner ran right up to Malvena and gave her the flowers from Osgar, which delighted the lass, no end. Then he told her Osgar was dead. It took a dreadful moment or two for the truth to dawn on her and as it did so, tears began to well-up in her eyes, trickle down over her comely cheeks, and drip one by one onto the purple blossom now clutched tightly to her bosom.

As the salt laden tears fell onto the heather, something quite remarkable happened: the purple colour was washed away from the flowers. For many weeks after receiving that terrible news, Malvena would rise early in the morning, often before the sun, itself. Having dressed quietly, she would wander away into the lonely glens and secluded places, to be alone with her grief. And, whenever Malvena became overwhelmed by her sadness, she would stand and gently weep for her lost love. Each time, wherever the tears were shed onto the purple heath – the colour was washed out of the flowers. The story tells us that, if you find yourself out on a moorland, at the time of the flowering of the heather, and you see, amongst the endless swathes of purple, a patch of white heather, you should pick a small piece and wear it on your clothes. It is well known that all the great fortune, which totally eluded that beautiful woman during her lifetime, is to be found concentrated in the blossom of wild white heather.

Malvena never found another love. She stayed at home and looked after her father, year after year. No doubt, they brought comfort to each other as they grew old together but because Ossian was wearing the golden ring of eternal life, he outlived Malvena and all his children. In fact, Ossian outlived many, many generations of his own family. Old beyond the counting of his years, Ossian was still roaming the world at the time of Saint Patrick.

24 Finn's Big Sleep

Finn MacCoul always enjoyed a good fight, but at the end of every battle he would be saddened by the loss of some of his closest and dearest friends. So Finn thought it would be just wonderful if you could have a fight and nobody actually got killed, so off he went to visit the Wise Women of Strathard. The Wise Women warned Finn that he should not interfere with the natural way of the world. But he wouldn't listen. However, they did owe Finn a few favours. So, reluctantly they gave him a kelpie skin bag, secured at the throat with a rope made from the bark of a rowan tree. Once tied inside - nothing could ever escape.

So, during the very next battle, instead of fighting, Finn went looking for Death. When Finn finally found Death, he really was delighted to see him. Death was just a bit surprised because nobody had ever been pleased to see him before – quite the opposite, in fact. Finn congratulated Death on organising such a magnificent battle: there were dead bodies everywhere. But now, he told death, he was so overwhelmed by hunger that he couldn't lift his sword for another blow. He didn't even have the strength to kill the little rabbit in his bag, to eat as a snack. Death, only too willing to help his new friend, called up a stoat to kill the rabbit. But the stoat refused to go into the kelpie skin bag. Then Death whistled up a wolf. But the wolf wouldn't go into the bag, either. Next Death summoned a golden eagle that swooped out of the sky, and promptly swooped away again. Even the bolt of lightening refused to do the job. So, Death decided that he would have to kill the rabbit, himself.

As Death leapt into the bag, made from the skin of a mysterious water-horse, Finn pulled out the rabbit and let it run free. Finn quickly tied the rowan-bark rope around the mouth of the bag. He had captured Death. The problem was finding a safe place to put him, where nobody would interfere and let him out again.

Finn decided to put the bag in the middle of the fierce hunting hounds, kennelled in a deep cavern under the hills of Gleann Dubh.

Battle after battle raged but nobody got killed. That was fine. People grew old, and still nobody died. That was alright. But there was no meat to eat – the animals could not die or be killed either. And that wasn't fine, at all! Finn realised he had made a serious mistake. Death should be set free.

Finn went into the kennel of the Fianna and brought out the kelpie skin bag from amongst the hounds. Untying the rowan-bark rope, Finn let Death loose on the hillside. Death went raging around the world, claiming all the souls that had been waiting for him to come. But, he kept well away from Finn and his people, just in case they caught him again and put him back in the kelpie skin bag. So Finn and the Fianna just got older and older, and weaker and weaker. Eventually, tired of waiting, Finn decided that if Death was not going to come for them, they would simply have to surrender. So, off Finn went to see the Wise Women. They were not very pleased with Finn, interfering with the way of the world. However, they still owed him a favour or two, and agreed to help him to take the Fianna to the next world.

The Wise Women offered Finn a map, enabling him to guide his people to Heaven, or he could have a map to take them all to Hell. Finn fully expected to find all his best friends carousing in Hell, so that is the map he took. There followed a very long march, with many wonderful adventures, before Cerberus, the three-headed dog guarding the gates of Hades, began barking his heads off. When the demons looked out and saw Finn and his people approaching the gates of Hell were instantly slammed shut.

Finn had in his possession a very useful bargaining counter – the kelpie skin bag. Once Finn had emptied Death out, he had abandoned the bag on the hillside but the kelpie skin bag began to follow Finn, keeping at heel like one of his hounds. Finn had a hole dug, and buried the bag but the bag came back. Finn then threw the bag into the dark river that flows through the heart of the glen, and watched it float away. A few hours later, wet and bedraggled, the bag was back. Next Finn took a boat out onto the waters of Loch Ard, filled the bag with stone and submerged it. It came back! Finally, Finn built a huge bonfire, with the kelpie skin bag right in the middle. After days and days of burning, when the mountain of wood had been reduced to nothing but fine ash – the bag was back.

Now the kelpie skin bag was going to prove very useful. Finn threw the bag over the high wall, deep into the depths of Hell. The demons didn't want it either, and threw it back out again. But they did agree to let all Finn's people, condemned to the ever-lasting flames, leave Hell and return to the Fianna. And to make sure they all went away, they gave Finn a map of the road to Heaven. Another long march ensued, with many more great adventures. One day, as Saint Peter was standing at his usual place just outside the Pearly Gates, he saw the host of the Fianna in the distance and the gates of Paradise were slammed shut. However, further negotiation saw Finn's take back all his people residing in Heaven and, with his nation now fully restored, they set off on their final journey – back to Earth.

The Fianna returned to Scotland and settled in Gleann Dubh, shut off from the outside world by a circle of mountains. Time passed, and Finn and his people got older and older, and weaker and weaker. And still nobody died. So Finn went off to the Wise Women once more. They gave him an almighty telling off for interfering with the natural way of the world. If Finn had listened to them in the first place, he would not be in this predicament. But, they did agree to help him, one last time. The Wise Women explained that the Fianna needed a good, long sleep in order to restore their lost vitality and vigour. And, to sustain them through this long slumber, Finn and his people would have to be adequately fed. So, the Wise Women prepared a feast.

The Fianna sat at the great banquet and stuffed themselves for seven days and seven nights, until not another mouthful of food could be swallowed by any of them. Rising from the still laden tables, Finn and all his people entered the underground caverns, hidden beneath the hills around Gleann Dubh, and fell into a long, deep sleep. And there they still slumber, waiting until they hear the clarion-call that will awake them – at a time when Scotland will have great need of their services.

25 Ossian's Ring

At the time when Ossian's wife left him to return to the Otherworld, flying away in the form of a crow, the greatest bard of the Fianna had been given a gold ring to wear – the ring of eternal life. Even though there was always an ache in his heart, Ossian continued to fight and hunt alongside his father, Finn MacCoul, living life to the full. At night, around the ceilidh fires, Ossian would recount the great adventures of the Fianna. Sometimes he would tell how his wife had come to him through a winter storm, transformed into a crow by an evil spell. Ossian would explain how the spell had been broken, and of the many happy years they had together, until that fateful slip of the tongue – the moment he called Niamh a crow.

In that flurry of Niamh's black feathers the light had gone out of his life. Ossian often related that part of the tale, but would never mention the ring of purest gold, which had been brought to him on the following day. The bard had put the ring onto the third finger of his left hand, the one that links directly to the heart, which is why it is the finger that a wedding ring is placed on, never, ever to be removed. In this way, although he grew extremely old, Ossian just did not die. He outlived his children and grandchildren and, after the time when the Fianna went under the hills to sleep, Ossian became the last of his race. For many years Ossian roamed the land, telling his stories and yearning for the times long past. Nothing was the same anymore. There was no sense of adventure in these puny people.

One day as Ossian wandered on, he saw a pure white horse grazing upon the heath. As he drew near he could see it was carrying a saddle of gold and wearing a bridle of silver. Once mounted upon the faerie steed, Ossian was carried across the land to the sea – and then over the tops of the waves. He beheld many wonders and strange places upon the water. At one of these places they stopped and Ossian, with all his strength restored, attacked a fierce Fomorian sea-giant to free a damsel in distress – none other than Niamh. With his wife mounted behind him, they galloped on. Ossian saw a hornless fawn leaping from the waves, pursued by a white hound with red ears. By the time they reached *Tir na Og*, the Land of the Young, Ossian was once again a young man.

Ossian stayed a while in the Land of the Young, until he had a great wish to see his own country again. Niamh put him upon the faerie steed and Ossian rode away from the daughter of Mannan Mac Lir, Sea God and first king of the Isle of Man. Ossian had been told that if his foot so much as came into contact with the ground, he would never be able to return to the Otherworld. Back in his own land he found everything changed. The bard enquired about Finn and the Fianna and was told that these were names from a bygone age, whose deeds were still recounted by storytellers. The Fianna had long been asleep beneath the hills, and Saint Patrick had come to Ireland and made all things anew. Even the shapes of the people had changed, there were no more people over 7 ft tall as the Fianna had been. After all, Ossian had been away almost 200 years.

Patrick had been one of a number of British children seized by pirates and carried off to Ireland. Slave trading was common practice. It was during these formative years that Patrick developed a love for Ireland and the Irish people. He did, however, manage to escape from his captivity and eventually make his way home to west Wales. Patrick received some education, but never to any high degree, and trained for the priesthood. Patrick spent some time in France before returning to Ireland to serve under Palladius, who was sent to be the first bishop of the Irish in AD 431. Patrick succeeded Palladius as bishop and based himself at Armagh. There is much more to Patrick than the priest who drove snakes out of Ireland or used the shamrock to explain the Holy Trinity. He accomplished immense missionary works of conversion that would otherwise have taken generations of evangelists to achieve.

This, then, was the land and the time in which Ossian found himself. He rode around the countryside taking in all the new sights and information, and wondering if there were any big people left in the world. One day, on seeing a number of men struggling to raise a stone slab, Ossian dismounted to lift it up for them. No sooner had his first foot touched the ground than the faerie horse vanished, and Ossian became a withered old man. It was in this wizened state that Ossian first met Saint Patrick. The bishop was as anxious as anyone else to hear the wonderful stories of the old bard. Patrick was so taken with these tales that he began to write them down – the first permanent account of stories of the Fianna.

Night after night the priest would listen avidly to tales of great adventures, making notes from which he could later write up full accounts of battles and hunts, and heroic contests – in Latin. The work would have been long and laborious due to his lack of higher education. Later scholars would describe Patrick's style of writing as rustic and inelegant. Ink was made from clear fountain water, left to cover a root of yellow-flag iris for 24 hours. Then, in the water, which had been boiled a little, a white pebble of quartz was rubbed onto a piece of iron. Within an hour the water became very black with a good ink. Using a goose wing-feather quill, Patrick recorded the tales of Ossian onto fine parchment of calfskin.

However as the stories became evermore incredible Patrick

became frustrated. One night, after hearing of a time when there were birds the size of deer for men to hunt, Patrick sent Ossian away and put the entire manuscript onto the fire convinced that these tales were no more than the ramblings of an old man's imagination. Fortunately, the bishop's housekeeper had made up the fire for the night, covering it with a thick layer of damp peat. As soon as Patrick had retired to his chamber, the girl quickly recovered the precious pile of vellum, quite undamaged apart from a slight scorching on the bottom sheets. Although illiterate, the girl realised the immense value of her master's work, and she took them home to the safe keeping of her family – to be passed down through the generations.

Ossian, now blind as well as extremely frail, returned to the New Ireland beyond the sea. Out of a sense of obligation to the old man Patrick had sent one of his own servants as a ghillie to the old bard, to tend to Ossian's every need. With the coming of winter, Ossian took to his bed, and didn't stir until spring. On the first really warm day of the new season, the ghillie helped his master from his bed. He suggested a bathe in the river might make the old Fiannan feel invigorated and refreshed after his long lie-in. They made their way slowly to the water where the ghillie un-dressed and washed the old man, until only the skin beneath the ring required to be cleaned. Without the slightest fuss, Ossian allowed the ring to be removed. No sooner had the ring been placed on a stone on the bank of the river, than a crow swooped down and carried it away!

Dressing his master in the new clothes he had made through the long winter months, the ghillie returned Ossian to his bed. The last of the Fianna, now well into his third century, soon fell asleep – a sleep from which he never awakened. I am sure that the ghillie sent by Saint Patrick was also a priest, and that at the very end Ossian had been baptized into the new faith. Ossian's grave lies in the solitude of the Sma' Glen, in the hills to the west of Perth.

The Scottish poet, James Macpherson, born 1736, came across Patrick's original manuscript. This provided the source material for his 'Poems of Ossian,' published in 1765.

Saints

THE LONG ESTABLISHED trading links between the Mediterranean states and Celtic countries quickly brought Christianity to Britain. The new doctrine sat easily amongst the pantheon of ancient beliefs, rapidly assimilating Celtic elements into Christian practices. The most important of these was the shared importance of sacred fire and holy water. Throughout history, ruling families had always provided the connections to the spiritual world. The Divine Right of kings only ended with the execution of Charles I, beheaded in 1649. Early Christians were steadfast in their faith and, in the second century, the veneration of saints began – after death. The first official canonisation by the church was recorded in AD993.

As the Roman Empire crumbled, barbarian hordes ravaged the civilised lands with nunneries and monasteries proving easy pickings. Celtic Christians simply travelled south to fill the vacuum left by their massacred brethren. This may well explain why the first three popes, after St Peter, were British; St Linus, son of the Brythonic chieftain called Caratacus, followed by St Anacletus and St Clement. The turmoil of the early centuries of the Christian Era brought the bones of St Andrew to Scotland and took St Fiacre and his comrades south, to France.

26 Scotland's First Patron Saint

Not only do we have stories passed on through the generations, but customs and traditions as well. Two of these customs are particularly relevant to hill shepherds. Firstly, when making myself a new cromag, or shepherd's crook, it was important to remember to put a small piece of silver or a small sliver of gold in the join between the tup's horn handle and the hazel shank. This is for exactly the same reason as any matelot serving in Her Majesty's navy is permitted to wear a gold earing – to be sure of always having the ability to pay Charon, the ferryman of the dead in Greek mythology, to row you to the next world.

The second practice is equally significant. When my time comes and I get a sudden call from St Peter, it is imperative that some-one remembers to put a small tuft of wool in my hand. Because, when I get to the Pearly Gates, and St Peter takes down the Ledger of Life and turns to my page, when he sees my poor record of kirk attendance, I could be in deep trouble. Then, if he notices the wool, and realises that I have been a shepherd, he will welcome me in a broad Scottish accent and direct me to the nearest bar. Paradise indeed. Not many people seem to be aware that Peter was patron saint of Scotland long before his brother, Andrew.

The earliest Christian missionaries to reach this land came with the Romans. Not the invading forces of AD79, intent on conquest and plunder, but the Roman traders who had been peacefully doing business with the Celtic fringes of their empire for a great many years. This would explain how Pontius Pilate was indeed born in Perthshire, at a place called Fortingall. Pilate's father was an officer in the Roman army, stationed in central Scotland to protect the trading posts. Some people would have you believe that Pilate's mother must have been a Scot. That cannot possibly be true, for two reasons; at this point the Scots were still living in Ireland and, secondly, a Roman officer would not have been allowed to marry a woman who was not a citizen of the empire. We were many things in north Britain, but never citizens of Rome.

The titular head of the Roman Church in those far off days, as now, was Peter, and Christianity managed to gain a foothold amongst a whole plethora of Roman deities and Celtic divinities. This was a time of relative peace and prosperity. The main trading involved the export of valuable metals, of which the Mediterranean lands were short, in exchange for Roman produce, principally wine and white wool. Celtic sheep only grew dark wool, servicing haute couture with any colour you like – so long as you liked it black. But white wool could be dyed in a full range of wonderful colours, making it a very valuable commodity. Four thousand years ago, according to the Book of Genesis, Jacob took as his pay for 14 years labour, all his employer's sheep and goats with any white in their coats and not to mention two of his master's daughters as his wives. There are several Old Testament stories about the ways Jacob increased the percentage of white fibre produced by his animals, but whichever way it was done, it brought him enormous wealth. Britain was renowned for the superb quality, if rather dowdy colouring, of its sombre clothing. The introduction of white wool would change all that as multi colours became very fashionable. Taking advantage of the ability to dye wool so easily brought about the creation of colourful fabrics, the most famous example of which is the traditionally Scottish Tartan. In fact the earliest reference to tartan is from Ireland, when, in 979BC, the High King made it a capital crime to wear a tartan to which you were not entitled. In Britain, much of the imported wool was spun, woven, dyed and turned into top quality garments, to be sold throughout the empire. In the Capitol, itself, you were nobody unless your toga carried a label proclaiming British origin.

Under the auspices of St Peter, the Christian faith became established in northern Britain. Time marched on. Pontius Pilate left these shores, embarking on his life of infamy. Having washed his hands of the fate of Jesus, he later died by his own hand on a lonely French hillside. After 400 years of occupation the Romans returned to Europe, leaving Britain to the Dark Ages. Through the turbulent centuries Christianity, somehow, managed to hold on, often quite precariously. This would explain why neither of the great Celtic saints, Ninian nor Columba, became Patron Saint of Scotland – the position was never vacant. Events started to conspire against St Peter in the fourth century, a time when the Roman

Empire was riven from within by internecine conflict and assailed from without by barbarian hordes – of which Scotland was just one.

It is at this turbulent point in history, that the bones of St Andrew, brother of St Peter, began their journey to Scotland, from Patras in Greece, for safekeeping. And that is the next story.

27   Saint Andrew

Andrew was born in Bethsaida in Galilee and, with his brother Simon Peter, became a fisherman at Capernaum. Initially a disciple of John the Baptist, Andrew was to be the very first of the 12 apostles of Christ. Carrying out his ministry at home and abroad, this missionary zeal made Andrew a great many enemies. In AD60, whilst preaching in Achaia, an area of southern Greece, the apostle was imprisoned by the Roman authorities, and then sentenced to death by crucifixion. The standard cross of crucifixion was made of two opposing stakes driven diagonally into the ground, upon which the victim was affixed. The cruciform construction so familiar to us as the cross, to which Christ was nailed, required more timber and would have cost more to make and so wouldn't be wasted on Andrew even if it would have given the large crowd a clearer view of the gruesome proceedings.

The actual site of martyrdom was the small town of Patras. After his death, the bones of Andrew were distributed between the local churches and the houses of the nobility, who would keep such things as good luck charms and talismans. This was a Golden Age, so much so that in AD67 Nero entirely suspended Roman supervision of the region. But as time slipped bye, dark clouds began to gather on the horizon. The great Roman Empire declined into turmoil as the powerful families struggled and fought for control, and barbarians battered the very gates of Rome. No-where was safe, certainly not Patras.

At this time, it was the duty of a monk named Regulus (*in English that would be Rule*) to safeguard the sacred relics of Andrew and see that they came to no harm. As the troubles rumbled on, one dark night Rule dreamt of an angel who came to him with a message. Rule was told to collect up all the bones of St Andrew, put them into a strong wooden box, place them onto an ox cart and ride away. The angel pointed north by northwest, and told the monk to keep going until he was told to stop, even to the ends of the world.

Slowly the ox cart trundled across the continent of Europe causing quite a stir. The passage of this box of bones met with much excitement. People came from miles around to marvel and, occasionally, steal away with a valuable relic of the old apostle. Some bones were left at Constantinople; a few, including the skull, were taken to Amalfi in Italy. By the time Rule's wooden box arrived at its final destination, it was a minor miracle that there was anything of Andrew left at all. If we were to believe the claims made for possession of these relics Andrew would have had more than 10 fingers, at least three shoulder blades and an unusual number of knee bones. Well he was a saint.

The last stage of this odyssey was by sea, probably leaving from somewhere between Denmark and Holland. Despite the duration of journey, made relatively short by favourable winds and tides, which made trading links between Scotland and the rest of the world possible, Rule's journey was not easy. His ship foundered off the east coast but somehow the monk, his trusty ox and the remaining relics made it ashore, on what is now known as the East Neuk of Fife.

At this point the angel returned, telling Rule to build a church, into which the sacred bones of St Andrew were to be laid. The angel also said that this would be a good place to build a golf course – but that is another story.

This explains how these holy relics arrived in Scotland carried by a monk on a holy mission, away back in the fourth century. But it is only half of the story of why, later, Andrew was to become Patron Saint of this country.

Four centuries slipped past and nothing much happened in the East Neuk. The original wooden church had been replaced by a stone edifice, grander in scale and design. A trickle of pilgrims, including the odd monarch, came to worship at the shrine, but nothing of moment occurred. That is until the eighth century, when King Athelstane of Northumbria marched north at the head of a large army of Angles and Saxons intent on conquest. Having hastily mustered as many fighting men as they could, the Pictish King, Angus, and Huw the Poisoner, King of the Scots, joined forces to face the invaders. They prepared to engage the enemy about 15 miles east of Edinburgh.

As the two armies lined up in battle formation under a clear blue sky, two long, thin, white wisps of cirrus cloud drifted overhead. Suddenly, right above the battlefield, a white diagonal cross appeared, the sign of St Andrew, as it was the shape of his crucifixion cross, whose bones lay just across the Firth of Forth. To the Picts and the Scots this was a great omen. To the Angles and Saxons it was a portent of doom – how right that was to be! The invading forces were completely massacred; even King Athelstane fell in the battle. The dead from both sides were buried together at the edge of the battlefield, close to where the River Peffer flows out to the sea.

A settlement grew up with the river running right through the village, taking its name from the slain Northumbrian King, which became known as Athelstaneford. The nearby county of Angus, also got its name after this battle. It was named after the Pictish king who, with his ally Huw the Poisoner, achieved a victory against overwhelming odds. After this victory, the local people quickly adopted the symbol of a white diagonal cross on a sky blue ground and, to this day, fly the saltire in front of the church at Athelstaneford. The saltire, from the French verb to jump and the Old French *sauteour* – an x shaped barricade over which you were required to jump, was soon adopted as the flag of the Scottish people. The flag of the Scots monarch is, as it was then, the red lion rampant on a yellow ground, to which the *fleur-de-lys* have been added around the border, in memory of the Auld Alliance with France.

The saltire of St Andrew is in fact the oldest national flag in the world. After this significant victory over the Northumbrian army, in which the symbol of St Andrew undoubtedly played a great part as it encouraged the Picts and Scots while completely demoralising the Angles and the Saxons, the cult of the apostle began to grow. By the turn of the millennium, St Andrew had become the most significant saint in the Scottish calendar. It was at this time that Andrew became a home grown patron saint, replacing his own brother, Peter, who had held that position for almost 1,000 years.

It is rather strange that these two brothers, fishermen of Galilee, without any outward connection with this remotest northwestern country, have each in turn become our patron saint.

28 Saint Columba

Horrified witnesses stood transfixed as the heavy cudgel smashed the life out of a small girl, leaving her thin skull crushed like an empty eggshell. The only voice was that of a young boy, a novice standing among a group of monks, who stated for all to hear that the child's soul was already bound for Heaven. The man, who had so mercilessly beaten his victim, only paused long enough to listen to his own fate as the boy intoned that the wrath of Almighty God would fall upon him and he would suffer the great tortures of everlasting Hell. Turning to flee from the scene of his crime, the villain fell screaming and writhing to the ground. People drew back in horror and when, at last, the body lay still, thick, dark blood was seen to be oozing out of every orifice. Whatever the given name of that young novice monk, from then on he would be known as Colum Cille. Surprisingly, Colum Cille means Dove of the Church. However, the Celts often referred to a person by using a name exactly opposite to their disposition, Colum Cille was certainly no dove!

Now known as Columba, he has become one of the most distinguished Celtic saints. Columba was of royal Irish blood, his mother a granddaughter of the King of Leinster and his father descended from the great Niall Ui Neill, High King of Ireland. His mother, Eithne, was told about Columba's coming by an angel, long before his birth, and St Buite, an obscure Irish monk and follower of St Patrick, foretold his power and influence. Training under two saints called Finnian, Columba showed exquisite skills and deft penmanship. Penmanship skills were particularly prized and admired because it was only these learned men that could copy manuscripts and many precious documents would have been entrusted to their care.

Having borrowed an extremely rare and original Coptic Gospel from his mentor, St Finnian, supposedly to read and study, Columba made a secret copy. When this misdemeanour was uncovered, St Finnian demanded that the copy be handed over. Columba was unwilling to part with the work of his own hand on the parchment pages, made from finest calfskin, and bound in the very best leather. With no settlement in sight, the case was referred to Diarmid, the High King of Ireland. The judgment handed down, in this first ever copyright dispute, was that as every calf must go with its cow, every copy must go with its book. At the announcement of this decision the darkest side of Columba became clear: he would not concede.

Through his royal bloodlines Columba had an enormous power base. Rather than give up the beautifully illustrated tome Columba was prepared to go to war. After all, like many holy men of his time, Columba was a warrior priest. The battle, fought at Cuildreimhne, County Sligo, was a bloody affair. Hundreds of brave men were slain. Columba led valiantly from the front but, finally, faced defeat. This last gamble had failed. Columba was now to be banished from Ireland, ordered by King Diarmid to live out his life in a place where his emerald homeland could never be seen. With a handful of men and very few belongings, except a young white horse, who as a foal, had wept tears on the monk's chest, Columba set sail to the northeast to a land already colonised by his own people.

Columba and his companions made frequent landfall on the far side of the sea, edging ever northward. From each point Ireland would still be within sight, until they reached Iona, one of the islands of the Inner Hebrides. From the highest hilltop, even on the clearest day, Ireland lay beyond the far horizon so Diarmid's order had been obeyed.

There was a second reason for establishing his base on this Atlantic rock: it was already a stronghold of the druids. Originally called I Iubhair (*pronounced as I Yoo-ur*) meaning the Island of Yews. Yew trees were venerated by the ancient Celts and believed to be immortal. The longest-lived of all British trees the Fortingall yew was already 2,000 years old when Pontius Pilate was born close to its shadow. The Christian faith happily adopted the Celtic belief that the yew was the guardian of the Door of Rebirth and signified rest after the struggle of life. To this day, yew trees are found in many old cemeteries.

The written form of Columba's new home was altered simply by inverting the letter U, making an N. So *Yoo-ur* now sounded like *Yoo-nr* or *Iona*, adequately disguising any links to the old religion. In AD565, two years after arriving at Iona, Columba set out on a new mission – to convert the Pictish people. With his royal blood, Columba would not start with the common men and women, and work up as was the way of other missionaries. He would start at the top, with the king – and then work down. Making their way through the Great Glen on the way to see the Pictish King in his Inverness stronghold, Columba and his comrades came upon the funeral of a young man who had been savaged by a great beast from the nearby loch. On hearing that this was a frequent occurrence, Columba went into the water and faced up to the creature, scolding it so severely that, from that day on, the monster of Loch Ness has never hurt another human being.

On arriving at Inverness, Columba and his colleagues found the massive wooden gates shut against them. King Brude, on the advice of his druids, would not meet the Christian monks. He soon changed his mind when Columba commanded the stockade to open – and it did! There then followed a contest of power and magic between the two religions, ending with a sacred flame lit by Columba, a fire that the druids could not extinguish. Faced by the evidence of its superior power many of the people, including the King, embraced the new Christian theology. There was, of course, much common ground between the two doctrines. In fact, Christianity adopted many of the old Celtic festivals and practices and turned them to their own use.

Columba soon cultivated a political power base in Scotland, becoming a leading adviser to King Conall. In AD575, along with Conall's successor, Aidan, Columba negotiated independence from the Irish control of taxes and military service. The Scots would, however, provide and maintain a fleet of ships for Ireland, built of best pine upon oaken frames and pinned with nails made from the heartwood of the sacred yew. This was a very good deal! Columba also managed to rebuild his power base in Ireland, even though he was officially banished. Founding Kells and developing it as a monastery renowned for producing magnificent manuscripts, Columba continued to illuminate work of his own. Only a portion of one of his psalters, book of psalms, and three divine poems survive, all in Latin.

On the sabbath, 9 June AD597, this remarkable man announced that it was to be his final day on earth. He took one last walk to the nearby hilltop, facing towards the land of his birth, gazing across the empty expanse of sea. From Gartan in County Donegal, Columba had travelled far in his 76 years – in more ways than one. He returned to his chapel and knelt at prayer until midnight, when he died. An Atlantic gale enraged the seas for many days and nights so there were no mourners at Columba's graveside other than the monks of the abbey, and his old white horse who wept tears onto the soft earth.

29   Saint Fillan

This story starts in seventh century Ireland. Kentigerna (*which can also written as Caentigern and Quentigerna*) was a daughter of Cellach, King of Leinster. The princess married a local warlord, who went about his business doing what warlords do – and got himself killed, which is surely an unavoidable occupational hazard for someone in his position. Kentigerna, now with three young children, faced three possible courses of action. She could kill herself, joining her husband in the next world, but who would care for her children? She could remarry, which had distinctive advantages: Anyone with the ability to take on an additional family would certainly be wealthy – and probably very old. Or her final choice, the one she took, was to take the veil, spending the rest of her life as a nun.

After she took her vows, Kentigerna, with her three children and her brother, a monk known as Comgan, set sail for Scotland, a land occupied by Irish emigrants, to become missionaries.

The Scots are descended from Scotia, a daughter of the pharaoh of Egypt, who married an Irish prince, bringing with her the true Stone of Destiny as part of her dowry. From a great-great-grandson, called Eber Scot, a whole nation has taken their name. The Picts, the indigenous people of what is now known as Scotland, made the newcomers welcome, seeing them not as raiders but as settlers. The Picts bestowed many gifts on the Scots, including the gift of women but with one proviso: The ruling dynasty of the land held by Scotia's men had to pass through the female line, preserving the line of Pictish blood.

The new kingdom of the Christian Scots expanded rapidly, at the expense of their largely unenlightened neighbours. Kentigerna and Comgan were just two of a great many missionaries who worked tirelessly amongst the uninitiated Picts. Kentigerna and her three children finally settled with a small community of nuns, long established on one of the islands at the south end of Loch Lomond. The Scots had quickly arrived, occupying the entire West Bank, and all the islands on the loch. Monks had established a monastery on their island, Inchtavannach. Across the loch, the nuns set up home on Inchcailloch, the island of cowled women. The holy men, however, ruled the roost, even controlling the time of day as they had the only bell in the area. The monks would toll their great bell to summons all the inhabitants, nuns included, to prayer time.

The advance of the Scots settlers came to a halt at Loch Lomond. With a surface area of 27.5 square miles, it is the largest sheet of freshwater in Britain. The water, and the mountains beyond, proved to be quite impenetrable. The expansion, however, continued apace around the north of the natural barrier, annexing land they named Atholl – meaning a new or second Ireland.

After the Scots almost completely settled the area Kentigerna, and many other monks and nuns, took their faith to the east, into the lands of the druids where their missionary skills could continue to be useful. Kentigerna's mission to the far side of Loch Lomond is commemorated in the name of the church at Inversnaid. Even after her death in AD733 her good work continued through the efforts of her child Fillan, who was dedicated to following in the footsteps of his mother and uncle.

After leaving the community of women on Inchcailloch with his family, Fillan, like all male children of this time, would have come under the tutelage of his uncle Comgan, before returning to Ireland for more formal training once he came of a certain age. It is believed that Fillan took Holy Orders at Taghmon, a monastery in County Wexford. Little is recorded of him from that point onward until he was discovered to be a solitary monk at Pittenweem, working amongst the Picts of Fife. For a short time Fillan served as an abbot, before resigning and retiring to the moody mountains of Breadalbane.

Breadalbane translates as the High Country of Scotland, and here Fillan settled, at a small monastery strategically placed at the heart of Glen Dochart. This is one of the principal routes to and from the Lowlands, used by man since time immemorial, which is generally agreed to be any time before AD1189 and the reign of England's Richard 1. Fillan became renowned for his wisdom and lack of fear, living up to the meaning of his name – Little Wolf. But it was his power as a healer that sets this Fillan apart from 15 others with the same name. Hearing of his miraculous healing powers many came to Fillan to be cured, especially from forms of madness. Close to the monastery run the waters of the Tay and it was in a pool in this river that Fillan affected most of his cures. Known as Saint Fillan's Well, the water retained its powers for more than 1,000 years.

During the twilight of his life, Fillan set himself the task of translating the Word of God into the language of the people, Gaelic. Working from Latin, Greek, Hebrew and Early English documents, Fillan laboured over his project, writing day and night in his small cell. It is said that, to facilitate this holy work, God gave Fillan a left arm that glowed brightly in the dark, which allowed the monk to illuminate his manuscript in more ways than one. Following Fillan's death in AD777, the fluorescent arm was removed from his body and kept as a sacred relic, becoming one of seven attributed to this saint.

After his death life at the monastery continued much as before. There was nothing of moment until the early 14th century. In AD1306, Robert Bruce, having been crowned King of Scots, had been roundly defeated by the forces of England's Edward I. With his army scattered and pursued by the enemy, Bruce sought sanctuary in Glen Dochart monastery. During this brief respite, Bruce was quite taken by the sight of the mummified forearm – still shining for all to see.

For eight long years Bruce waged a guerrilla war against the occupying power. By the summer of AD1314 things had come to a head. Only Stirling Castle remained in English hands, and after a long siege the English had agreed to a pact that if they were not relieved by Midsummer Day, then they would surrender; all would be lost and Scotland free. Edward II, the weak son of Edward I who had died in AD1307, marched north at the head of the largest English army to come across the border on business. While awaiting the enemy Bruce sent for the arm relic of Saint Fillan, now lodged in the more luxurious surroundings of Dunblane Cathedral. Not liking the odds of Scottish victory, the monk in charge had ignored Bruce's orders to send the relic to him on the battlefield and had left it in the safety of the Cathedral. Imagine his shock when it reappeared when the ornate casket was opened at Bannockburn! The rest, as they say, is history. The small Scots army, supported by a squadron of Knights Templar, completely macerated the Auld Enemy.

With the capture of the English baggage train and the ransoming of their survivors, Scotland became the fourth richest country in Europe. Against impossible odds, through the intercession of St Fillan, Bruce had triumphed – Scotland was a free nation once more.

30 Saint Fiacre

Saint Fiacre, born around the beginning of the seventh century, was a Scot who has become one of the most important French saints. Nearly every study of Saints claims that Fiacre was an Irish monk. However, by this time, there were more Irish living in the territory known as New or Second Ireland, which is now Scotland, than in the Emerald Isle so it is safe to call him a Scot. Like all newly emerging nations there had been rapid development and vigorous expansion. The two leading centres of religious life and learning were on this side of the Irish Sea. Whithorn, founded by St Ninian in the fifth century, was an important Christian enclave in British Galloway. Iona, on the other hand, advancing under the guidance of Columba, now stood at the very heart of this new kingdom – Scotland.

It is thought by many that before the modern times travel must have been severely limited but this is wrong. From earliest times Celtic druids were known to have journeyed as far as Tibet, if not further. The ropes of horse hair, goat fibre and pig bristle, on which the cragsmen of the remote collection of islands named St Kilda entrusted their lives, have been found in the high Himalayan mountains and nowhere else.

So for Fiacre and a few fellow monks to make their way quite easily to mainland Europe is not surprising. From the days when the power of Rome was at its height, wave after wave of barbarian hordes swept over these lands, raping, looting, burning and pillaging as they went. The people were slaughtered and their country laid waste. Men and women of the Church were not exempt; in fact they presented soft targets and rich pickings. As fast as these monks and nuns were butchered, others willingly came to take their places so serving the people of the war torn country. The Roman Empire shrank beneath the incursions of Huns, Vandals and Goths. Finally the Visigoths stormed through the south of France and into Spain – and stayed. These were difficult times.

It was exactly into this situation that these monks from Scotland arrived, in AD626. Fiacre offered their services to the bishop of Meaux, a few miles due east of Paris. The Scots were told that they could settle on as much land as they were able to enclose with a plough in one day. The bishop expected Fiacre to yoke an ox to a heavy, single furrow implement, slowly marking out the boundary of their new holding. One long day of sweat and toil should provide adequately for their needs. But Fiacre was a man in a hurry. Choosing his starting point, the monk placed the tip of his hand-held staff on the ground in front of him, and began to walk. Never lifting the tip of his staff from the ground, the earth simply opened up into a furrow, as deep and as straight as anyone had ever seen. At Fiacre's pace, an awful lot of ground was going to be enclosed that day! However, it was not going to be quite that simple.

A local nun was not overly impressed by this minor miracle. Nor was the bishop when he was told of the situation. His Grace made it absolutely clear that he didn't care how ploughing was done in Scotland, here, in France, it was going to be done with an ox, and an old one, at that. Perhaps after the betrayal of that nun Fiacre developed a sudden loathing of women. From that day onwards, not a single human female was to come into his sight.

After his reprimand Fiacre built a hermitage and settled to a truly monastic existence, which was ideal for Fiacre. Priests and druids were the learned men of the day – the fount of all knowledge. In the case of the druids, everything was committed to memory. At least Christian priests were able to write and record their information for posterity. Even then, some things were closely guarded secrets. Fiacre brought many skills to France but he also gained a lot of local knowledge.

The brethren grew much in the way of produce, not only for

food, but a great many herbs and plants for their medicinal properties. It is for this reason that Fiacre is the patron saint of gar-
deners and horticulturists, and is often depicted with a spade in his
hands. Many of the remedies that he and his brethren produced
would have been brought from his homeland and used since pre-
Christian times. The healing properties of sphagnum moss, collected from the peat bogs of the north, would be desperately
needed in that troubled period. Gaping wounds were simply
packed with dried sphagnum, the moss absorbing any discharge
and promoting rapid regeneration of the flesh. Frontline field
dressings are still based on sphagnum. In France, Fiacre would
have come across many new plants and their associated therapies
only increasing his reputation.

Fiacre was the also the student of many other skills such as
adding the mysteries of wine making to his skills of brewing ale
and distilling whisky, monks maintained their monopoly in this
particular field for many centuries to come. Fiacre was also one
of the first Europeans to know something else – how to knit. It
was not until the return of the surviving crusaders that knitting
became widespread. Garments could now be produced more simply and much quicker than by felting or weaving the wool. It is
hardly surprising, then, that Fiacre is also the patron saint of the
French Stocking Knitters Guild.

From its earliest days the Celtic church had developed in
splendid isolation much as Fiacre flourished alone, and the influence of a huge number of their saints is testimony to the vigour
of their ministry. But the Church centred on Rome was on the
march and although there was much common ground between
Celtic and Christian religions, there were also major differences.
The main sticking point was the calculation of Easter and the
preceding period of Lent. The old rhyme about Jack Sprat eating
no fat and his wife eating no lean, is about an Anglian king and
his Celtic queen going into their Lenten 40-day fast at different

times. Even here the Roman Catholics had changed things, giving themselves one day a week off from the fast. Their Lent stretched to 46 days. There were no such shenanigans in the Celtic theologies, but their Golden Age was coming to an end.

There was a shift in power towards Christianity that wouldn't be stopped and men like Fiacre were leading the people.

Significant Travellers

IT IS A COMPLETE misconception that worldwide travel is a recent phenomenon. Our ancestors were known to be globetrotters, druids roving as far as Tibet and returning with wonderful stories. Further evidence can be found in the technique of producing special rope from horsehair, goat fibre and pig bristle, on which the lives of St Kilda men frequently hung. It is identical to the ropes only found in the high Himalayas. And the maze, turned into a fine garden feature by Capability Brown, is mentioned by Homer's *Iliad*, written well before 700BC. Until recently, the Celts used the maze for a practical purpose, to protect the peace and privacy of a newly married couple. A complex pattern would be drawn at the entrance of a honeymoon house, preventing any malevolent spirits getting inside and upsetting the newly weds.

There are countless stories of significant travellers, many coming across the world to Britain, some leaving these shores to find adventures in far flung places. Thankfully, these selected stories are still being told.

31   Jesus' Visit to Scotland

This is a story given to me on my first visit to the Long Island of Lewis and Harris, in the early summer of 1973. As a botany student I had been lucky enough to make the acquaintance of a local crofter. Hamish was only too pleased to show me the carpet of wild flowers that stretched over his machair, as far as the eye could see. The seemingly endless strip, just out of reach of the sea, was ablaze with colour. As we stood, ankle deep in orchids, watching the huge Atlantic breakers rolling in, I listened to Hamish's story.

Nearly 2,000 years ago, when the machair looked just the same as it is now, Jesus came to that very spot on his Hebridean Tour. He was strolling along the vast expanse of sandy beach, communing with nature, when he became aware of imminent danger – his enemies were closing in. Jesus was completely exposed, there was absolutely no hiding place. Two oystercatchers, seeing their Lord's predicament, flew to his aid. They told Jesus to lie down on the high-water mark, where the wet and dry sands meet. Then they quickly placed bits of seaweed and wrack on and around his prostrate form, breaking up the outline of his body. Staying close at hand, the two birds began dibbling in the sand, as if looking for their food.

The adversaries, intent only on doing Jesus great harm, rushed across the machair, over the sand dunes, and onto the windswept beach. They looked this way and that, but could see nothing but the great Atlantic waves – and two birds with jet black plumage and long orange beaks and pink legs. This was surely the wrong beach, and off they hurried to search elsewhere. When it was quite safe to do so, Jesus got to his feet and brushed himself down. He thanked the two birds that had undoubtedly prevented his life on earth coming to an earlier end than the one already planned. Jesus blessed the two black oystercatchers, giving them the white cross so characteristic of the species today: an indelible reminder of their great service to Christ.

This was a simple story simply told, but sounded as fresh as if it had happened the previous day, not as though it was a story that had been passed on for almost 20 centuries. It is a great example of the oral tradition. Hamish had given me the story in all sincerity, and I had no reason to doubt the truth of it. But it wasn't to end there.

Sixteen years later, in South Wales, I met up with a biblical scholar. Not only was this priest interested in my story – he had a bit more to add.

This story was to explain the apparent visit of Jesus to Scotland, which sounds to many so unlikely. It says that Mary, mother of

Jesus, who it seems, was not just a virgin but a Temple Virgin, chosen because of her great purity. A pregnant Temple Virgin was quite a problem – enter Joseph the carpenter. The first 12 years of Christ's life are well documented but, after he had preached in the Temple, the next 18 years are a bit of a blank. It is believed that around this time Joseph, being considerably older than Mary, died. As is still the custom in that part of the world, Jesus and his large number of brothers and sisters would have been cared for by close relatives. And Jesus was adopted by his uncle Joseph of Arimathaea, Mary's brother.

Joseph was a rich merchant who traded widely, even to Britain. For many centuries, long before the conquests of Rome, there had been a great deal of trading between the Mediterranean countries and the Celtic fringes. Joseph of Arimathaea was many times at Glastonbury, in fact he is the Patron of the Somerset town. If Jesus was apprenticed to his uncle, isn't it more than likely that he accompanied the merchant on these trips? William Blake, in his famous hymn, 'Jerusalem', asks the rhetorical question, 'And did those feet in ancient times... walk on England's green and pleasant land'. Obviously, there is a tradition in that part of England that he did.

Even now the story of Jesus' visit to Scotland is not finished. Another piece of the jigsaw was about to fit into place. An ocean going yachtsman, with vast racing experience, assured me that from the west of Britain the best way back to the Mediterranean was to sail in a clockwise direction. This would explain why the very first maps of the British Isles show Scotland tilted towards mainland Europe. It was evidently as quick to sail from Aberdeen to Antwerp, as to voyage between the Hook of Holland and Hull. Without the aid of instruments the ancient mariners mistakenly equated sailing time with distance. So the possibility that Jesus made a landfall on the Long Island grows ever stronger.

But there is more. I remembered from my dim and distant

days of studying zoology, there are oystercatchers with all black plumage. On checking with the Royal Society for the Protection of Birds, this was confirmed. They also told me that the population of oystercatchers with the white cross on their feathers appears to be centred on the island of Harris and Lewis. Another amazing coincidence. Unless, of course, the first oystercatchers to carry this distinguishing mark lived and bred on the Long Island, some 2,000 years ago.

Jesus lived to fulfil his predetermined destiny. After his brutal crucifixion Jesus' body was placed inside the tomb belonging to Joseph of Arimathaea. Tombs were the prerogative of the wealthy. They were expensive to excavate out of the solid rock, but provided certain protection from grave robbers and marauding wild animals looking for food. Joseph's tomb could not, however, offer any security against angels – but that is another story!

32   The Devil's Visit

If Jesus could come to Earth in human guise, why not the Devil himself? There are many such stories to be found in the Scottish Highlands, some strange, a few quite astonishing – all of them spine-tingling. When the new faith of Christianity came north to Orkney, Loki, the Nordic demon, was recognised as the fallen angel of the Old Testament – Beelzebub, a biblical name meaning Lord of the Flies. The Devil soon came to reclaim these converts to Christ, but their allegiance was too strong. On the parapet of the ruined church near Overbister, on the island of Sanday, the Devil's lichen encrusted finger marks can still be seen. These were said to have been wrought into the stone in sheer frustration by Auld Nick, as his words fell on deaf ears.

On another occasion His Satanic Majesty turned up at Thornhill, in Stirlingshire, to do a deal with Robert Napier. The famous alchemist had been searching for the secret of everlasting life. The

tryst took place at Ballinton House. On failing to reach agree-
ment, the Devil leapt from an upstairs window and disappeared
into the night.

At Kilneuair in Argyll, stands the ruins of St Columba's Church,
formerly the parish church of Glassary. Built at a time long before
the Highland Clearances, the stone for the church was said to have
been passed hand to hand from the quarry at Loch Fyne – 10
miles away. Imprinted on the door-frame is the Devil's handprint,
where it had been impaled by the tailors bodkin, a thick needle
for making holes. The tailor was sitting in the doorway, sewing
an ornate altar frontal piece, when the Lord of Darkness came
for his soul – but the tailor had other ideas on the matter.

The infamous Aleister Crowley (1875–1947), who described
himself as the wickedest man of all time, was for a while the laird
of Boleskin, on the shores of Loch Ness. Judging by the number
of stories, Beelzebub relishes the challenge of playing cards with
foolish mortals. One night, at Boleskin House, the Devil made up
a foursome within a locked room. Crowley was the only survivor
– and even he was not prepared to say what had taken place. At
the moment of Aleister Crowley leaving this world from his home
in Brighton, on 1 December 1947, a tornado swept through the
town – accompanied by great peals of thunder that sent shivers
down everyone's spine.

There are many tales of the Devil's visitations but the most
fascinating story about the Devil concerns the time that he came
to Strathard, looking for souls to claim for his Kingdom of Fire
and Damnation. There he discovered Gog and Magog, the last
British giants, sleeping under the spell of the McAlpines – the local
Wise Women. The Devil thought that it would be a great idea to
wake them from their long slumber and turn them loose once more.
It is not that Gog and Magog were in any way dangerous like
other giants, they were just clumsy. Well, very clumsy. So, eliciting
the services of a coven of witches from the Kingdom of Fife,

where all the wickedest witches live, the Devil and the witches prepared their plan of mischief.

At the appointed time, under cover of a moonless night, the wicked witches took off on their broomsticks. Moments later they arrived, quite unseen, alongside the Black Master. There, on the south shore of Loch Ard, the Weird Sisterhood began to work their powerful magic. Strange incantations wafted into the night air, to be carried away on the wind. The darkness deepened, becoming so thick that the stars above could no longer be seen. A tawny owl shrieked and the Essence of Gog and Magog began to seep out of the ground. Their Essence, in the form of a grey mist, trickled over the ground in two small streams, flowing towards the unsuspecting people of Aberfoyle slumbering in their beds.

Deeper into Strathard, the persistent cronking of bible-black ravens, in the dead of night, had alerted the McAlpines to the fact that there was evil afoot. Guided by the pricking sensation in their thumbs, the Wise Women of Strathard soon found themselves at the scene of the mischief. The wicked witches from Fife didn't want any trouble so, when they saw the McAlpines approaching, they jumped onto their broomsticks and disappeared off into the night – leaving the Devil to face the music, all on his own.

The leader of the local witches immediately launched an attack upon the Evil One. She was nothing if not fearless! I am told that this mistress McAlpine was a large, very strong, and extremely ugly woman – with quite a temper, too. The furious witch leapt upon Beelzebub. She punched him, scratched and clawed him, pulled his hair and poked his eyes – and did a few other things that ladies should really never do to a gentleman. The Devil, trying to defend himself from this ferocious assault, resorted to the old demonic trick of making his skin burn as hot as fire and brimstone. The witch, using her considerable powers, made herself bigger, heavier, stronger and even uglier than she had been before. It was becoming quite a fight.

At some stage in this brawl, with mistress McAlpine's enormous thighs clamped firmly around his neck, the Devil managed to regain his feet. Now, carrying the witch piggy back fashion, the Prince of the Night fled up the strath – him getting hotter and hotter, and her getting heavier and heavier. On and on he ran, past the darkened dwellings of Kinlochard, and on to the ford crossing the River Forth. However, once the Devil had gone down into the shallow water, he couldn't get out the other side – not with that great weight on his shoulders. Turning to his left, the Lord of Hellfire splashed his way upstream, billows of steam spurting out from beneath his feet. If you follow the river west from where the fine stone bridge crosses the water, here and there, you may chance upon a demonic footprint in the bedrock.

Meanwhile, back at the south side of Loch Ard, where the two giants had begun to stir, the rest of the Wise Women were getting things back under control. Using their great magic the McAlpines were re-setting the spell, cast upon Gog and Magog by their ancestors 200 years before. The Essence, not liking to get wet, had oozed eastwards along the shoreline. Silently it drifted past the Duke of Albany's old keep, standing forlorn on a small islet. Sadly, without the care of its former custodians, Gog and Magog, the fortifications were being brought down by the ravages of time. Suddenly there was water directly in front of the two rivulets of smoky spirit, not yet restored to flesh. Unsure as to which way to go, the Essence gathered into two grey columns. Behind them the McAlpines; in front the expanse of water and the coming of the dawn. At this point the haze solidified into two pillars of solid rock.

Fortunately, at some point during their flight through the upper reaches of the strath, the Devil and the witch came to an understanding. She would let him go on his way, without further molestation, providing the Devil gave his word never to return to Strathard. As far as we know, he never has.

The Forestry Commission have cleared away the trees from around the two grey columns, and they are now clearly visible from the B829 on the opposite side of the loch.

33 Ebenezer Erskine

Scotland has only one natural lake, the Lake of Menteith. It received this English title in 1305, when John Stewart of Menteith betrayed William Wallace to the forces of Edward 1 of England. The people were so incensed by this inordinate act of treachery, from that point they would only speak to John Stewart in the English language. They also began to call everything about him by an English name, taking away John Stewart's Scottish loch and replacing it with the derogatory term, lake.

The Erskines have held lands in Menteith as far back as records and memory can trace. For several centuries the first born son to the Erskines of Menteith has been given the biblical name of Ebenezer, from Hebrew *eben ezer* – meaning stone of help. Many of these Ebenezers became ministers in the Church of Scotland. The Ebenezer Erskine of this story was born in 1680, died in 1745, and is famous for three things. First of all, in 1732, he led the Great Disruption of the Church, when he and a few of his ministerial colleagues stormed out of the General Assembly in high dudgeon and set up a breakaway movement.

Secondly, Ebenezer Erskine believed that God had intended him to preach the definitive sermon against the Demon Drink. For many years he wrestled with his topic and how to speak about it so that everyone would listen. He spent so many sleepless nights wrestling with the words, to no avail. Then, one Wednesday it was, he left his manse at the top of the town of Stirling on his way to visit an alcoholic shepherd who tended his sheep on the great morass that, long ago, completely surrounded the capital of Scotland. Later that day, as Ebenezer made his way back to the manse, Divine

Inspiration came upon him. In an instant the whole sermon congealed in his brain. He could hardly contain himself until the Sabbath. On the Sunday morning he raced through the early part of the service until at last it was time to mount the steps into the impressive wooden pulpit in the Kirk of the Holy Rood, standing in the shadow of Stirling Castle.

To this day, people still talk about that wonderful sermon, more than two hours of tremendous passion and enormous endeavour. But this being Scotland, I am afraid Ebenezer Erskine completely failed in his objective – the taverns, inns and bars are still open for business.

The third thing that Ebenezer Erskine is famous for is the fact that he was conceived and born five years after his mother had died – and had been buried in her grave. Truth, it is said, is often stranger than fiction. The story begins a few hours after the November afternoon funeral. The weather conditions were atrocious, with flurries of driving snow and horizontal sleet. The funeral party had not tarried long at the open graveside, hurriedly returning to the shelter and comfort of the nearby manse.

The minister, having just buried his lovely young wife, was so distraught that he had shut himself away in his study. The parlour maid hadn't even gone in to turn up his oil lamps, leaving her master to grieve alone. As the unhappy widower stood in the gathering gloom, gazing out of the window in the direction of the church and the ground where he had just buried his dead wife, the early winter darkness tightened its grip. Suddenly, the minister's heart must have stopped beating, if only for a moment. Walking towards the manse, lit by the light coming from all the other windows, was the woman he had just laid to her Eternal Rest!

The poor man, also Ebenezer by name, closed his eyes and went into deep and fervent prayer, thinking he had simply gone mad in his distress. And when, a few moments later, through his prayers, his courage began to return, he opened his eyes and looked out but there was nothing to be seen. He was just telling himself that it had been no more than a momentary hallucination, when there was a banging and clamouring at the door of the manse. The minister rushed out of his study, knocking the parlour maid clean off her feet in his haste to get to the door. Wrenching it open, into his arms, wet, muddy and dishevelled, but very, very real, fell the woman he had so recently buried.

They carried her through to the parlour, laid her gently on the chaise longue, and examined her in more detail. The only injury that Mrs Erskine seemed to have sustained, during that terrible ordeal, was a missing finger. But really she was missing something more than that. The sexton, the man overseeing the funeral arrangements of the minister's young wife, had realised that Mrs Erskine was going off to meet her maker, dressed in her finest clothes and wearing all her jewellery to her grave so had gone back under the cloak of darkness, uncovered the coffin and opened it. Quickly, he began to collect the valuables.

Everything was fine until he got to Mrs Erskine's wedding ring, which was such a tight fit it wouldn't come off. So out came his clasp-knife, off came her finger – and up sat the minister's wife! Mrs Erskine scrambled out over the unconscious body of the sexton and made her way home to the manse, where she made a complete recovery and lived to raise a family of 10 children. Her first born son was, of course, given the name Ebenezer.

This tale may seem incredible but the truth is often stranger than fiction and there is evidence to suggest that this story may have more than a grain of truth in it. Just a few years ago, in Leeds, a woman called Maureen Jones collapsed and died. A police officer was in attendance as an undertaker prepared the body for removal to the mortuary, prior to a postmortem examination. The young officer thought he detected signs of life, but the undertaker explained that this was quite normal. Gases are formed inside the body, sometimes causing occasional noises, and even slight movement. But the policeman was adamant that the route to the mortuary would be via Leeds Royal Infirmary, where, three days later, Mrs Jones regained consciousness. The unfortunate lady had simply lapsed into a catatonic trance – a condition not unknown to medical science.

34 MacGregor's Potion

Young Robert MacGregor was one of a great number of Highland Scots serving in the British army, and seeing plenty of action against the French in North America. A grandson of Rob Roy, Robert MacGregor had taken the King's Shilling and left Balquhidder to seek his fame and fortune. The British were casting envious eyes at French dominated North America, wanting to add that great landmass to their rapidly expanding new Empire. General Wolfe, having served in Scotland, had learned his lessons well. Not only did he take Scottish regiments with him to America, his land forces were being led by Cameron of Locheil – a man said to be more fierce than Fierceness herself.

However, during a small skirmish, MacGregor and six of his comrades fell into the hands of a Huron scouting party, a Native American tribe fighting with the French, and were taken prisoner. At the tepee encampment, the soldiers soon found themselves securely confined inside the only log built lodge. They spent a very uncomfortable night, hoping that Locheil would send troops to rescue them. At first light, the door burst open and a handful of warriors grabbed the nearest redcoat, dragging him outside as he kicked and screamed. Then, unseen but certainly heard, their victim was slowly and horribly tortured to death. The second night in that log cabin was even more uncomfortable than the first. Rescue seemed a far distant hope.

As the first light of dawn filtered through the tiny cracks in the walls of that windowless cell, the door flew open and in poured the bloodthirsty natives. But as they overpowered another soldier, MacGregor stepped forward and said, '*Vous ne voulez pas faire ca*'. Meaning, 'You don't want to do that', in those days the second language of a Highlander would have been French. '*Mais oui – On veut le faire!*' replied the Huron, allies of the French, replying that they certainly did want to do it. But the tribesmen paused just long enough for Robert MacGregor to offer them a deal.

He explained that his own grandmother had been a shaman, a powerful witch doctor. If the braves would release his companion, and only if they released him, then this grandson of a shaman would make them a powerful potion. It would be an ointment that, when rubbed onto the skin, offered complete and perfect protection against anything made of metal. No blade of steel; neither lance, spear nor arrow tipped with metal; no bullet or musket ball could do them any harm. This quite excited the Huron, and the relieved soldier was returned to his comrades.

Each day, under heavy guard, MacGregor wandered through the forests, selecting the occasional plant from here and there. The longer he could spin this out, the greater the chance of being rescued. It was pleasant enough being out of the cramped hut, he could stretch his legs and breath the pure summer air. Even the biting black flies were not nearly as bad as the midges back home. The young Highlander quickly perfected the art of delaying tactics. He explained that some plants, essential to his grandmother's recipe, had first to flower. The flowers would need to set their seed, and the seeds have time to fully ripen – nature could not be hurried.

Summer began to turn to autumn, and there was still no sign of rescue. The nights were not just getting longer, but very much colder, too. As the first snow settled on the mountain tops, and the Huron began to get a little bit impatient, MacGregor decided to go on to phase two of his plan. Time to get cooking. In a sheltered spot at the edge of the camp, close to a small stream, MacGregor selected the site for his fire-pit. From the available clay and metal pots, he fashioned an array of strange looking cooking utensils. Just like his grandmother used, he said. This, of course, took up a great deal of time. As did collecting just the right kind of firewood. All the while the six surviving redcoats were praying to be rescued.

With the first heavy snowfall of winter, all hope of rescue had to be abandoned until next spring. Robert MacGregor spent the short, cold days huddled over his fire, baking, roasting, braising, with quite a lot of boiling, too. Every evening, just as darkness fell, MacGregor would make his way back to the lodge, carrying what the Huron took to be a beaker of water. It was no such thing. From the fermented liquid, produced by the collected seeds, nuts and grains, MacGregor was able to distill raw spirit – alcohol. This certainly made the passage of the freezing and interminably long nights a great deal more tolerable.

At long last, the days began to lengthen. Once again the Huron were getting restless, but the Highlander had one last card up his sleeve. He had got his potion, what the prisoners needed was more time. There could be no rescue attempt before the snows melted. In the bottom of his home-made still was a thick gunk that pretty well solidified overnight. MacGregor ordered a new clay pot to be fired – and more time passed. When it was ready, the special pot was filled with great ceremony. First MacGregor further reduced his concoction, boiling it off in a shallow pan. Then, to the amazement of the elders of the tribe, as the white man poured what they took to be water into the simmering pan – it burst into flame! Even their own shaman could not burn water!

As a final flourish Robert MacGregor even flambéed the filled jar, before sealing it with a layer of buffalo fat. The potion now had to mature for three full cycles of the moon. That would take them into May. If they had not been saved by then...

The first moon waxed and waned, as did the second, and still no rescue. The helpless captives watched the third moon run its course and vanish. There was great excitement throughout the camp as the fourth new moon appeared high in the afternoon sky. MacGregor calmly announced to his captors that he would demonstrate potion, on himself, at sunrise. Time was fast running out.

All night long the British soldiers waited in vain. Help, it seemed, would never come. At first light Robert MacGregor strode out of the log cabin, clutching his jar of magic ointment, and walked to the clearing in the centre of the settlement. The place was absolutely packed. Every warrior for miles around had come to see this demonstration of paleface power. Procrastinating to the last, MacGregor slowly undressed. He then washed himself all over and, finally had his beard neatly singed. Still there was no sign of rescue. Taking the pot and removing the layer of buffalo fat, the young Highlander rubbed the ointment all over his skin. The moment had come.

Without the slightest qualm, MacGregor knelt down and put his head on a large wooden block. An enormous Huron brave stepped forward, a mighty warrior with a mighty tomahawk. The steel head of the tomahawk came crashing down on the soldier's neck – sending his head rolling into the crowd. There was a stunned silence! To a man, they instantly realised that they had been duped. Once over their shock, they began to appreciate the great bravery of this man, who was prepared to lay down his own life to buy time for his friends. As a tribute to MacGregor's selfless sacrifice, the Huron not only released the remaining five captives, but returned them safely to the British lines. And so the soldiers told their story, passing it down through the generations, for you to hear.

35   Cesare

This is a story about a daughter of Noah called Cesare. Although the Bible does not mention Noah having any daughters, only three sons, Shem, Ham and Japhet, and their wives it does not deny any daughters, either.

A long time ago, after the Great Flood had abated, and after

371 days in the Ark, Noah and his people brought the animals out onto the dry land. And God put a rainbow into the sky as a sign that He would never again bring a flood to destroy mankind. The untamed animals returned to the wild and the people tilled the soil, planting crops and tended to their herds and flocks. Everything was much as before, except there was nobody else around. Soon the pattern of the seasons had been re-established, and every living thing set about obeying God's command – to go forth and multiply. All of them, that is, except Cesare.

Noah's daughter was a rather prissy little madam, who would not even consider a relationship with any of her surviving male relatives. So, after a great deal of consideration, it was decided to send Cesare out into the world to seek her own fortune. In their spare time, Noah, Shem, Ham and Japhet built a new ark – something they were quite good at. This rather smaller vessel was, of course, constructed at the seaside. Masses of timber had been washed-up all along the shore, so it didn't take them very long. Once the ark was ready, Cesare was put on board. She was given enough animals to provide her with food, such as milk and eggs, during her voyage, and to be her dowry – should she ever need one. And Cesare was sent on her way, sailing towards the west.

After many weeks at sea, Cesare eventually made a safe land-fall. She was glad to get ashore from her small ark, to stretch her legs and find new supplies of food and fresh water as it hadn't rained much lately. But this did not look like a place to settle down in, so Cesare re-boarded her boat and sailed on. Over the next few months Cesare landed here and landed there, but could never find a place that she wanted to make her new home. Just as she was beginning to think that she might have to spend the rest of her life on her crowded little ark, another land came into sight. On going ashore, Noah's daughter found this to be a green and very pleasant land. In fact, it was ideal. At long last, the animals were able to disembark.

Cesare had not been given any of the young animals, bred since the end of the flood. They were far too valuable to part with. Noah had given his daughter only the remnants of his old stock, some of them animals of great age. Nevertheless, they had provided well for Cesare during their long journey across many seas. Now, grazing their new pastures, their coats soon began to shine. They, too, would begin to multiply. Cesare, a very able young woman, quickly stripped down the superstructure of the ark. What had been her cabin at sea became her new house on land. Meanwhile, unknown to Cesare, there were other people in this country – descendants of Ith, son of Bregon, first settlers on this land. In no time at all, word of her arrival spread far and wide.

The local warlord came to see for himself, and he liked what he saw. Here was a presentable young woman, and her animals constituted a considerable dowry indeed. When the warlord turned up to pay court to Cesare, and wouldn't take no for an answer, Noah's daughter resorted to an old biblical trick. Hurling her wooden staff onto the ground, it instantly changed into a large snake and chased the unwelcome suitor away. The disgruntled warlord reported the matter to his chieftain, who also came to see for himself. He, too, liked the look of Cesare and her fine animals, and decided to take possession of them all. But when he arrived with six men to carry her off, Cesare's staff changed into seven snakes and chased them all away. Cesare was quite fussy in her choice of a husband.

This situation just went on and on. Next came the governor of that province, and, after him, the prince of the region. In a matter of weeks, Cesare was fast running out of possible husbands – and the whole country was being overrun by snakes and serpents! At last, the High King of that land came to see what all the great excitement was about, and who was letting loose all these horrible reptiles. The High King also liked what he saw and dearly wanted to take Cesare as his wife. Having run out of chances, and possible husbands, Noah's daughter realised that unless she agreed to marry this man, she would have to pack-up again and sail away. And, this time, Cesare quite liked what she saw.

There are many stories telling us that all the children of Ireland are descended from that union of Cesare, daughter of Noah, to the Ard Righ of that country. It goes without saying that they both lived for a very long time, and happily ever after. Many years later, Saint Patrick turned up and sorted out the problem of all the snakes that Cesare had used to chase away her suitors, ensuring that, once again, Ireland was a land free of snakes.

Witches

WITCHCRAFT IS SURPRISINGLY prevalent in the 21st century. Even today there are apparently ordinary people who have extraordinary powers, an ability that comes upon them quite naturally. Royal Naval records contain an authentic report about the news of the death of Queen Victoria being taken to a remote Shetland island, 11 days after the event where they found that the islanders were fully aware of the exact time and all the details of her late majesty's demise: the Wise Woman had told them. Their vessel was the first to call at that island for at least six months.

This final selection of stories are all about witches, concluding with the tale of the very last witch to be imprisoned for her supernatural knack.

36 Good Witches

A long time ago, the Wise Women of Strathard lived in their tiny cottage close to the bank of the River Forth. Strangely, it was the only house in the entire community of Kinlochard that was separated from all the other houses by the river. Witches, of course so the legends say, cannot cross running water, and if these were wicked witches then the people of Kinlochard would have been protected by the river. But these particular witches had never been known to be mischievous or malevolent in any way, and their help and advice was sought by many people. Their fame and reputation were second to none. One of their ancestors had taken part in a contest of witchcraft and magic against Merlin, the greatest magician of them all. Another had wrestled with Satan himself, and lived to tell the tale. And they themselves had cast a spell to put the giants Gog and Magog to sleep. So, when Rob

Roy MacGregor asked for help in finding some stolen cattle, it was no bother at all.

The MacGregors were one of the clans living along the edge of the Scottish Highlands, charged by the government to protect the livestock of their rich, Lowland neighbours. For many years these well fattened animals had provided easy pickings for marauding clans from the north. The payment for this protection service, set by law and paid in cattle, was called blackmail. It was simply an insurance scheme. There was not much use for money in the Highlands, you could not plant it to grow or cook it to eat. The principal unit of currency was in cattle, shaggy black cattle. The red-coated highlander cows, so prevalent today, are the product of a double recessive gene for colour, popularised by the Victorians. Originally a payment in black cattle, blackmail now means coughing up under a degree of duress.

The Earl of Lennox had called out Rob Roy's Glengyle Watch to retrieve 30 head of prime, fat stock lost by his tenants. It was expected that 30 cows would be returned, even if they were not the ones that went missing, no questions asked. Two young trackers were dispatched to pick up the trail. An experienced man could recognise signs left by a drove of cattle for up to ten days. Once the route had been established, one of the trackers would return to the main party and the pursuit began in earnest. The Watch would be well trained, well organised and certainly well armed. With the full backing of the law, a Watch could go anywhere and take any action required to recover their quarry. Once back in the Highlands – they were the law.

The trail of Lennox's lost cattle led northwards, along the west bank of Loch Lomond and into MacFarlane country. There were clear and firm rules to the business of rieving livestock and it was never considered as theft – not in the Highlands, anyway. In those times people viewed cattle very much as we look on wild red deer today. God had provided these animals for all his children, and they should be distributed according to individual need. There was a great deal of redistribution going on. Once a missing drove had been tracked into a clan territory, that clan were required to prove that the animals had left their land, or it was presumed they had stolen the animals and they had to make good the loss. Another reason for ensuring that the cattle had passed out of their area was that they received a payment for allowing them through. This was known as collop.

Rob Roy's trackers had easily followed the trail into the heart of MacFarlane's mountainous country, but were struggling to find the exit route. Each blade of bent grass and every broken twig was carefully examined. Soft ground was scoured for footprints; high passes of exposed, weather scoured rock surveyed in detail, to no avail. The way pointed out by MacFarlane's men was anything but convincing. However, MacFarlane assured Rob Roy that the animals had long gone. Rob Roy had got detailed descriptions of some of the missing stock, one of the animals being distinguished by her mottled hide. Whilst MacGregor was receiving the usual hospitality from his Highland host, including some fine beef said to be collop from the Lennox cattle, his scouts were busy at work. There were 30 beasts, somewhere.

With no sightings of the missing cattle amongst the MacFarlane herds, Rob Roy decided on a different ploy – ask the Wise Women of Strathard. Visiting their dark abode, the captain of the MacGregor Watch explained his problem. In the meantime, 30 head of his own stock had been sent down to the Lowlands, to compensate the Earl of Lennox for this loss. He wouldn't get them back unless he found the original cattle. As Rob Roy sat in the gloom, under the soot encrusted cruick beams, the women stirred to their task. They would use xylomancy, divination using sticks; oak for knowledge, yew for truth, ash for clear sight and rods of hazel to point the way. No rowan. Witches don't like the wood of mountain ash, which is another name for rowan, because it is thought to protect people from magic. The twigs were mixed together and dropped onto the hard beaten earth floor. In the light of the flickering peat fire in the central hearth, casting strange shadows around the bare stone walls, the MacAlpine sisters, the Wise Women of Strathard, could see their answer.

Rob Roy and his clansmen returned to the northwest corner of Loch Lomond. Once again MacFarlane gave full permission for a thorough search to be carried out. Having accepted the customary hospitality at the chief's table, Rob surprised his host by ordering the new investigation to start inside the house – in that very room. Fires, even household fires, are sacred to the Celts, and should never be extinguished. Ignoring MacFarlane's protestations, the heart of his fire was lifted from the hearth and carefully placed into a hollow log, brought for that purpose. As soon as the fire had been safely removed, the hearth was cleared and the digging began. In no time at all, just as the Wise Women had said, the carcass of the distinctive mottled beast, still wearing its skin, was uncovered – packed in the preserving properties of peat. The game was well and truly up.

The rest of the missing animals were found butchered and hidden under the floor of a nearby barn, exactly as predicted. There was no loss of face; the game had been played within the accepted rules. Rob Roy made the short journey home, around the head of the loch, his men driving thirty head of fine MacFarlane cattle. This brought to an end another successful recovery for the Glengyle Watch of Clan Gregor, thanks to a coven of local witches.

37 Bad Witch

Everyone is born different from anyone else, that is what makes us all individuals. Some, however, are much more different than others. From the beginning of time there have been a few people that have come into this world with a special power – witchcraft. If these faculties are cultivated and nurtured, they can be developed into abilities far beyond the scope of normal beings. Whether used for good or evil purposes depends on the nature of the witch or war-lock concerned, but this is a story about a bad witch.

The heyday of practitioners of these Black Arts was during the turmoil of the 17th and 18th centuries, when Scotland was racked by civil war and Jacobite rebellion. At the collapse of each uprising, many of the supporters of the Stuart cause would have to flee the country, at least until the heat died down. The supporters of the exiled James VII were known as Jacobites, from the Latin word for James. His son, James Frances Edward, took up the cause and called himself James VIII. He went around pretending to be king when someone else was seated on the throne, and is remembered as being the Old Pretender. Life was not good to James Frances Edward; it was mostly spent wandering around Europe trying to drum up some support.

In the aftermath of the 1715 insurrection, a number of the leaders had fled to France with the Old Pretender rather than face imprisonment – or worse. This is how the Laird of Abergeldie found himself a long way from his Scottish Highlands. His wife, at home in her castle overlooking the River Dee, often wondered how her husband was faring in that far off land. In those days keeping in touch was almost impossible and she was getting very nervous about what he was up to. At last, losing her patience, the Lady of Abergeldie decided to consult the local witch. She was an old and evil crone that most people would not go near but these were desperate times calling for desperate measures. The lady was determined to find out exactly what the laird was doing in France. So secretly, she set off into the forest of Mar, a dark and forbidding place, following a stream that would guide her to the witch's house. It wasn't much of a house. The roof was made of turf, the walls were built from turf, the floor was bare earth, and the whole place was dark, dank and very smoky. The Lady of

Abergeldie stooped through the low doorway and entered into the one room. A peat fire glowed in the hearth, situated in middle of the floor, the smoke making its way out through the roof as best it could.

The witch was seated in the gloom, spinning wool from a black wedder on a drop spindle. Without looking up, she asked her visitor the purpose of this encounter. A deal was soon struck. For the price of two white woolled female sheep, as you know a fine rarity in those parts, the lady would learn all about her husband. Ashwood logs and scots pinecones were put onto the fire. Water was poured into a cauldron and hung from a chain over the flames. Soon steam began to appear, slowly filling the small room with mist. The witch wrapped a length of the spun black sheep's wool around a long twig cut from a yew tree, the tree of truth, and gave it to her visitor. The Lady of Abergeldie was directed to poke the stick into the fire, under the boiling pot, and observe closely.

As wisps of dark smoke from the smouldering wool spiralled into the grey mists, a scene in far away France came before her eyes. There was her husband, walking in the company of a beautiful woman whose red dress matched the rage in her own heart. The Laird of Abergeldie had no thoughts of Scotland, no thoughts of his lands – and no thoughts of his wife! The lady promised the old hag one of the best crofts in the whole of Aberdeenshire if she could bring this situation to an end, even to the cost of her husband's life. The new bargain was sealed; the witch would do as the lady asked if she could live at her ladyship's expense.

The old woman used her powerful craft to call Abergeldie back to his home. About the time he was to take a ship to Scotland, the witch prepared to make her way to the laird's own castle. Pouring a gallon, that's almost five litres, of water into her blackened, soot encrusted cauldron, she put it to boil over the fire. Into the seething pot the crone added secret ingredients, one after another. This time, the steam not only filled the tiny hovel, but flowed outside as a great, grey cloud. One gallon of water can be made into a square mile of fog, more than enough to cover her path to Abergeldie Castle. As the mist rolled down the burnside, filling the little valley and hiding the trees, the lady of the castle knew that the witch was coming.

Hurriedly making her own arrangements, as directed by the sorceress, the cheated wife realised that there was no turning back, her husband was doomed and she was playing her part. In a small garret room, right above their sleeping chamber, the Lady of Abergeldie waited with a fine French porcelain bowl, half full of water newly drawn from the River Dee. Afloat upon the water was a piece of wood, cut by her own hand, from her husband's side of the marriage bed. Now, she was to stand directly above his sleeping position, and hold the bowl steady. Somewhere, deep in the bowels of the castle, the witch began to bring her evil spell to its unholy climax. The water in the porcelain bowl started to stir and the sliver of wood danced on the surface. The water became even more agitated, until the bowl was difficult to hold on to. Suddenly, the fragment of wood broke up into tiny bits and disappeared into the maelstrom – at which point our lady fainted clean away.

Some time later she recovered, finding herself lying cold and wet upon the floor with the water that had soaked her tasting strangely salty. Of the witch, there was nothing to be seen and nobody else had known that she had been at Abergeldie Castle, or ever met its lady. Time passed and her ladyship began to regret her actions, hoping against hope that her husband was safe. News eventually came that his ship had been lost and that she was now a widow. Mad with grief and guilt the little farm promised to the old crone would never materialise, even if it was ever intended, instead the Lady decreed that the witch was to be burned to death, inside her own turf hovel.

The building, for all it was, was quickly reduced to a pile of ashes. There was nothing left save for the old cauldron, now more blackened than ever. There certainly was no trace of the witch. However, that very day, a strange old cat arrived at the kitchens of Abergeldie Castle, and lived at her ladyship's expense for many years to come.

38 The Wickedest Witch

On a large island off the west coast of Scotland, noted for spirits of all kinds, lived the most wicked witch that ever drew breath. Everybody feared the dreadful power of her magic, all mortal creatures avoided her presence and the trees would rustle at her passing – even on the stillest of days. The old hag lived in a small house on the outskirts of one of the townships, alone except for a sly black cat and a billy goat that gave her milk. She was often seen combing the goat's long, smelly beard, as if in deep conversation. By day a scattering of hens scratched around the house, roosting at night in the rafters. Nobody could ever guess how old the crone was, or how long she had been on the island – but they all thought it was time she was gone.

The problem was how to get rid of this extremely dangerous witch: the worst of her race. There was nobody brave enough to even consider such a course of action, never mind carrying it out, until someone came up with the brilliant idea of poison. After all, no freshly baked bread, cake or biscuits were safe if she caught even the smallest whiff. So, poison it would be. Very early on the next baking day, a large fruitcake was prepared, full of fine fruit and full of the deadliest poison. Just moments after being put out to cool, the cake had vanished. No one saw who took it, but everyone knew. For the rest of the day the people went about their normal business. Well, as normal as they could keep it, trying not to get too excited – not even daring to think what tomorrow might bring.

Early the following morning, when the people looked towards the sinister house, there was no smoke drifting upwards, no sign of newly fed hens, and the billy goat was waiting to be milked. It was still many long hours before a few of the young men summoned up enough courage between them, to peer into the dark interior. Yes! She was dead.

They found her body lying cold and stiff upon the hard earth floor. As the young men dragged the carcass of the witch through the open door, the hungry hens flailed and flapped into the daylight. While a grave was being dug, the hens clucked anxiously around the feet of the men, their breakfast long overdue. The witch was quickly buried, followed by a day of great celebration. The people of the island happily went to their beds that night, thinking that was that.

Oh, no it wasn't. The next morning the old witch was back – more wicked and more evil than she had ever been before. Panic spread through the people, what were they going to do now? Groups of frightened people gathered to discuss this dangerous state of affairs. There was a great deal of talking and quite a lot of drinking as of course it is widely held that drinking helps the thought processes. After the talking and fuelled by large quantities of whisky they decided on direct action. Suitably emboldened, a group of young lads rushed into the witch's lair, something they would never have done sober, and stabbed the old crone to death. Then they buried her and thought that was that.

Oh, no it wasn't. Before the sun had returned to the sky, she was back. And this time she was even more wicked and even more evil than she had ever been before. The islanders couldn't believe that they could have been so silly to think that they could kill a witch with brute force, after all everyone knows that, just like werewolves, the proper way to kill a witch is to use something made of silver. It just so happened that the Lord of the Isles was being served by an archer from Clan Gregor, a man by the name of Fletcher. His aim was so true, it was said that he could take a playing card from a man's hand at 200 paces. So, while it was still dark, Fletcher took his place behind a low stone wall, with a clear line of sight to the witch's house. At last, as the old crone came out through the door with her flock of fowls, the archer sent a silver-tipped arrow into her black heart. And down she went – stone dead!

This time they buried the old hag in the deepest hole that anyone had ever seen. All the men folk took a turn at digging. Great rocks and enormous boulders were piled on top of the body and a massive granite slab dragged over the grave. Surely, they thought, she was gone forever. No she wasn't! She came back; far more wicked and far more evil than she had ever been before.

A wave of sheer terror swept across the island. People hid in their houses. Even the Lord of the Isles cowered within Finlaggan Castle. Eventually, a new plan emerged. A large body of men gathered, rushed into the witch's house and stabbed her until she was quite dead. Then, to make quite certain, they stabbed her to death again. To make doubly sure that she could never come back, they chopped the witch into tiny pieces. Burying the bits at the bottom of the deepest grave of all, they covered the site with almost half a quarry of stone. At long last, the witch was gone. They congratulated themselves on a job well done.

But it wasn't. She was back. But this time she was everywhere, all over the entire island. Wherever you looked there were bits of the witch – a finger here; a kneecap there; or a bit of a toe hopping through the grass. If you felt that strange sensation of being watched, and turned around, one of her cruel eyes would be staring in your direction. This would never do. They had to do something quickly. Over the next few days, the islanders bravely picked up all the bits of the witch, gathering her into an empty whisky cask. A large bonfire was prepared, built from barley and oat straw, cut heather and old barrel staves. Once the fire had been lit, it was kept well fed with dried peat and more wood. Eventually the islanders recovered every last particle of the witch. Tightly nailing the oak cask shut with long iron nails, and with the local coopers adding extra iron hoops, the reinforced barrel was heaved into the flames.

The great fire was kept burning for seven days and seven nights, never left unattended. At the end of that time nothing was left of the oak barrel or its contents. Even the iron bands had melted away in the heat. At night people would gather, looking at the flames and watching the sparks spiralling up into the darkness. Some of the sparks came from the burning of the peat. Some sparks came from the burning of the oak staves. But some of the sparks came from the burning of the old witch. As these sparks drifted up into the night sky, cooling as they climbed, the witch cast up her last evil spell turning the sparks into thousands of midges!

The witch's spell has spread far beyond her island home, every summer tormenting people in many parts of Scotland. And to know that this is a true story, every biting midge is female – each one a tiny wee bit of the wickedest witch of all.

39   Travelling Witches

One of the great advantages of being a witch is an ability to get around and about, even to far-flung places, without too much bother. In the old days for ordinary people journeying was limited to walking or using waterways. For most, far away places would remain just unseen exotic names. Farmers often travelled to the nearest market towns to sell their produce. Fishermen left their homes to cast nets on the offshore waters. And some would do both. In the north and west of Scotland, where the land is hard and unyielding, communities were forced into harvesting the sea to augment a meagre return from the soil.

One day, long ago, MacIntyre and his three strapping sons set sail from the rugged west coast, expecting to take in a couple of days fishing. Behind them their ewes were all lambed and the crops newly planted and, with a fair wind at their backs, they looked forward to a pleasant time going after the silver shoals of herring. As the sun dipped into the Atlantic, the wind shifted a couple of degrees, just enough to cause the old father to get uneasy. By the time the ocean had swallowed the last of the light, the wind was lifting the sea into great rolling waves and driving their vessel into the darkness. In this area of many islands, rocks and reefs, it seemed that the full fury of the storm was about to claim new victims, four more souls to be consigned to the deep.

By a stroke of good fortune, the stricken boat was hurled up onto a sandy shoreline. But the danger was not over – far from it. Each new wave of the flow tide threatened to reclaim the ship and suck her back into the storm. Two of the sons plunged over the side, each taking a rope to secure their boat. The dangerous mission accomplished, they rode out the rest of the tempest. When the storm calmed they discovered that the ebbing tide left the fishing boat high and dry, her back clearly broken. Having no idea to which outpost of the world they had been delivered, their only option was to repair the craft. It was probably their only chance of ever returning home.

Leaving his three sons to look after the wreck, and guard her valuable timbers against thieves and looters, the father set out in search for the one straight oak needed to redress the fractured keel. Axe in hand, the old man walked through the forest. Trees there were a plenty, great stands of oak. But this was largely coppiced timber, trees grown and managed on a 24 year cycle. These young oaks provided tannin rich bark for curing hides and skins into leather. Their wood was turned into charcoal, to smelt iron and manufacture gunpowder. Trees grown through two 24 year cycles yielded ideal timber for house building. The few selected oaks, completing 72 years in the forest, were destined for the ship builder.

Not for their length, but for the natural angles found in the boughs. He needed to find an older, taller tree.

His quest for a suitable tree was seemingly never ending. This oak being tall enough but bent. Another standing straight enough, but far too thin. When he did find one tree of sufficient girth and length, standing proud and erect, it had been cracked by the very storm that had driven his boat ashore. Just as the day was fading, the stranded fisherman found himself at a small house in a clearing. Woodsmoke drifted from the chimney at the gable end of the building. This was quite a modern house, it was very rare to have such a chimney. A dog barked and an old woman came to the door, inviting the stranger to share their hospitality for the coming night. Inside, as his eyes became accustomed to the gloom, he saw a sister even older than the first, lighting a small cruse lamp. The weak, flickering light from the burning oil illuminated the wrinkled features of the oldest beldam of them all, seated crouched in a dark corner.

After a surprisingly good supper the guest was conducted behind a screen, into what passed for a bedroom. It was customary for such a visitor to take the bed for the night – even if it is the only one. The only other furniture, apart from a large bed, was a large wooden box or kist. After a while, when the women thought he was asleep, although he wasn't, the first of the sisters crept up to his bed. The terrified man could hear his heart pounding and the creaking of her old joints, although he kept his eyes tightly shut. The hinges on the box squeaked open, as though she had stepped on a mouse, and the weird woman lifted out a nightcap. Placing it on her head, she beckoned her two ancient sisters to come forward. Each in turn retrieved and put on a nightcap from the open kist. 'London', they chorused and promptly vanished.

On getting over his shock, the old man peered into the box, and found one last nightcap lying at the bottom. Pulling the woollen cap onto his head, he determined to follow the women, wherever they had gone. The word 'London' was hardly out of his mouth when he found himself once more in their company. He seemed to be in a well-lit cellar, although he had no idea where the light was coming from. There were no windows and the stone walls were lined with rows of barrels – barrels of beer, barrels of wine and barrels of finest spirits. And the three sisters had already started the party. In deference to their company, the old Highlander removed his headwear and entered into the spirit of things – literally.

He was kicked and beaten back into consciousness by a group of very angry men, yelling at him in an unintelligible language. Of his weird companions there was no sign. Confused and quite befuddled, he was half dragged, half carried away between two burly officers of the law. There were blurred images of a narrow stone stairway, a crowded street and a small, spinning room full of dirty, smelly people. And nobody spoke in his sweet Gaelic tongue. Roused from a fitful slumber, the poor old man was frog-marched into another room, a more formal chamber. Here, men in robes and wearing wigs were obviously discussing his situation, which, even in his state of mind and in a foreign language, appeared to be quite dire.

Dire wasn't really the word for it. In a few moments he found himself on a scaffold, facing a large crowd of onlookers, and standing beneath a gallows! He was to pay the price for all the drink that had gone missing from a securely locked basement. A crime unsolved for many years – until now. A priest spoke to the condemned man, first in English, then in French, Spanish, Latin and, finally, his own native tongue – Gaelic. The old man's last request would be to go to his maker wearing the nightcap still tucked inside his pocket, instead of the hangman's hood. As the white woollen cap was stretched down over his face, closely followed by the hempen noose, he bellowed, 'Lochaber'.

In an instant he and the entire scaffold crashed onto the beach, a stone's throw from his broken boat. The priest had been tipped into the crowd and the hangman had fallen off somewhere over

Kettering, but their old father had been returned safely, if in rather unusual circumstances, to his waiting sons. The gallows, quite undamaged by the heavy landing, was used to repair the fishing boat, and served as its keel for many years to come.

40 The Last Witch

The art of witchcraft is as old as time itself and, although sometimes feared, was generally accepted as a fact of everyday life. That was to change during the reign of Mary Queen of Scots, when such ancient practices were deemed to be a threat, both to the government and to the crown. The Act of 1563 would lead to some 3,000 charges of witchcraft over the next 173 years. Not all of the cases ended with the death of the suspect but a significant number did. The last witch execution took place at Dornoch in 1727. Eight years later, the London parliament greatly modified the old Scottish Act of 1563, but witchcraft was still recognised as a serious crime. Helen Duncan would become the last person to be tried for witchcraft.

Helen Duncan was born at the end of the 19th century, in the bustling West Perthshire town of Callander. The timeworn road and recently laid railway ran north from the town, quickly disappearing into the Pass of Leny, one of only four natural routes to the High Country of Scotland. Here the power of a highland river had slowly sliced down through the Highland Wall, thrust upwards when two enormous landmasses came together, more than 400 million years ago. The rocks themselves were altered by the impact. There was a considerable rise in temperature, resulting in re-crystallisation, and the formation of successive sets of fractures along which much movement took place as the rocks cooled.

Perhaps it is the energy stored in the reformed crystals, found all along the Highland Boundary Fault, which is responsible for a high number of strange manifestations and unusual occurrences.

Not only do things mysteriously appear, there are inexplicable disappearances, too. There are well-authenticated stories of people who have just vanished and, on one occasion, the entire Ninth Legion of the Imperial Roman Army marched into infinity – never to be seen again. It was here that Helen Duncan was born, in 1897, into a travelling family. The young Helen soon moved away from the area but the power imbibed at the place of her birth was with Helen Duncan for the rest of her days.

Whether Helen had any outside help in developing her powers is not known, but word of these amazing abilities spread far and wide. Soon she was conducting public meetings as well as attending more intimate gatherings. In those troubled times of the First and Second World Wars the services of Helen Duncan were much sought after. In all other respects she was a perfectly normal woman, marrying and producing a family of six children. During the early years of the Second World War, Helen attended an endless round of meetings and dealt with a continuous stream of visitors asking for news of loved ones. In 1941 she told a large audience about the sinking of a British vessel – before the official announcement. Now the authorities began to sit up and take notice.

There are a number of techniques that may be employed in the practice of divination. Helen Duncan favoured the use of xylomancy, reading the patterns produced by dropped twigs, a technique favoured by the Wise Women of Strathard. Wood is an old Celtic medium, still used by water diviners, conjurers with their magic wands – and orchestral conductors. But she also used less recognised methods and was able to bring out ectoplasm from within her own body. This milky white film could not only form itself into human shapes, but they would speak and answer questions. The police and naval authorities raided a small private meeting being held on 19 January 1944 where Helen and the three other participants were arrested. Helen Duncan was held without bail: the charges; vagrancy, fraud – and witchcraft.

The most damning evidence used against Duncan related to the sinking of HMS *Barham*, with the loss of 861 lives, torpedoed by U-Boat U331. If asked, a witch must give an answer, even if it is not what the questioner really wanted to hear. The sinking of HMS *Barham* was so serious a loss that the government invoked the Official Secrets Act, fearing the news of this loss would undermine public morale. However, Duncan had been disseminating this information to worried relatives before the authorities even knew what had happened to the ship. In court, a police officer gave graphic details of how he had tried to stop the flow of ectoplasm material emanating from Duncan's mouth. Whilst the prisoner had been restrained, he had continued to pull out this endless filmy substance, until his arms got tired and he was forced to stop. Helen Duncan even offered to demonstrate her powers from the dock. Not surprisingly, the court refused.

Found guilty of witchcraft, under the Act of 1735, Duncan was sentenced to nine months imprisonment with no appeal and no remission. All other charges were thrown out of court. There was, of course, a hidden agenda behind this whole charade – D Day. Early in 1944 the plans for invasion were being laid and Helen Duncan had to be removed from the streets for fear that she would release the secret plans. Amazing as it seems, one of her most regular prison visitors was the Prime Minister Winston Churchill – who can tell what went on at those clandestine conclaves. The invasion of Europe was, however, ultimately successful. Having briefly lost his power, in 1951 Churchill returned to 10 Downing Street. Almost immediately, Parliament repealed the Witchcraft Act and just three years later such practices became officially recognised as a religion – Spiritualism.

The case of Helen Duncan became a *cause célèbre*, especially following her release. Over the years there has been a campaign to reverse the verdict and quash her conviction. In order to head off the growing wave of concern and actually prove a case against her – any case – the police began to harass Helen Duncan. She was put under constant surveillance and subjected to frequent raids. There was never any evidence of malpractice or fraud, and no further charges were ever brought against her. As a direct result of a rather brutal sortie by Nottingham Constabulary, in November 1956, Helen Duncan ended up in hospital. And still there were no charges. On her release from hospital, Helen Duncan insisted on returning to Scotland, the land of her birth and source of her supernatural powers. Just a month later the newspapers announced the death of the last person to ever be convicted for witchcraft.

Afterword

THESE 40 STORIES WERE chosen with some difficulty from a vast repertoire, freely shared amongst a galaxy of storytellers. To my surprise, having completed the book, I find that these tales mostly fit into a band running from Antrim, through Central Scotland and eastward to the Kingdom of Fife. This, of course, is where I have lived for more than 30 years and collected these and many other stories.

When does any story become part of the oral tradition? Quite simply, when it is being told for the very first time. I hope that you will select a story to pass on snippets of information, as a cautionary tale for young listeners, or just for pure enjoyment – and become another storyteller.

If you are at all worried about the truth or accuracy of any story, you can always start your tale with the wonderful Gaelic disclaimer – 'If it is a lie that I am telling you, then its a lie exactly as it was told to myself'.

An Extract from *Red Sky at Night*

Chapter 1

THE STAR-SPECKLED BLACKFACED night of the first day of December begins to break as the light of the new day gently touches the eastern sky. Ice thickens and the white frost tightens its early morning grip. In the shelter of the drystone-dyked fank, the Glengyle tups, still cuddling on last evening's hay, begin to stir themselves, heads lifted high, nostrils held to the sharp edge of the wind. Beyond and above on the still dark hill, 38 score of ewes will already be foraging, hungry for the first bite of the short winter day, their ground about to be taken over by strong-horned mates. Dawn inches up over the night sky; a new year for the flock of the forked glen is about to begin.

Frost-crisped grass scrunches softly under my feet as I make my way to the fank. Alerted now, 16 tups tug long wool staples free from the frozen ground and scrabble to their feet. Four sheepdog muzzles push enquiringly between the lower spars of the gate; Old Bo, Mona, Gail and Boot size up the job in hand. At this intrusion the tups bunch tightly in the middle of the pen, their smoky breaths merging into a small, grey cloud. I pause at the gate, leaning over the top to study my charges, making sure that all is well before taking them out to the hill. Each tup in turn shakes himself vigorously, sending a shower of fine ice prisms flying and glinting into the first slanting shafts of sunlight.

The success, or otherwise, of the Glengyle flock in the coming year depends upon the performance of my tups during the next six weeks. Having satisfied myself that these fellows seem to be sound in wind and limb, I lift the snek and allow the wide wooden gate to swing open. Particles of white hoarfrost shower from the metal hinges. Three dogs dart inside to bring the tups out. Two or three heads turn defiantly to face up to the threat, but are quickly turned back again under the strong-eyed gaze of the collies. Guided out through the gate, across the bridge, a left flank by Mona and Gail turns the sheep to the right, and up through the park we go, towards the hill gate.

The sun lifts itself above the hills which fringe the south shore of Loch Katrine. The water sparkles. A small herd of whooper swans swims, dabbling for food in the sheltered, shallow lagoon in front of Glengyle House. A cold, north-westerly wind blows directly down the glen, bringing hints of ewes in season to the tups and a tingling to my fingers. Mona and Gail head off the tups and bring them to a halt. Bo and Boot guard against any retreat as I open the gate to the hill. Eager to fulfil their roles, 16 curly-horned heads turn onto the low-end of Glengyle. Last summer's lush bracken, burned brown by back-end frosts and battered flat by autumnal gales, crackles underfoot.

The hirsel of Glengyle covers almost four square miles, more than 2,000 acres and lies between the loch shore at 384 feet and Meall Mór summit, 2,451 feet above sea level. From the north-west, the Glengyle burn flows down the ice-chiselled valley into the dark, deep water of Loch Katrine. My ground stands to the north of the water which gives it the considerable benefit of facing south into the life-warming sun. Across the burn, on the aptly-named Dhu (Black-side), much of the ground does not see the sun for six long winter months.

Mountain grasses, together with bilberry and a little heather, provide most of the grazing on this rock-strewn ground. Each one of my ewes requires over two acres of pasture to secure sufficient food. Sheep do not just wander over the hills feeding at random, but have a firmly established grazing pattern. No matter how often a flock is gathered in, once they are returned to a hill, they all make for their own particular ground in the vicinity of their birth place. All the ewes are directly descended from long family lines. Each small family unit grazes over an area of 100–150 acres and, normally, is never found off this ground. Several units will co-exist on a section of the hill, their territories overlapping, forming a cut or heft of sheep.

It is to each of these hefts that I now introduce a tup, his coat dyed bright yellow to help me to see him from a distance, as I walk my daily rounds. The traditional number of tups for Glengyle is 16; six on the low-end and 10 on the high-end. The number of tups put out is critical. Too few, of course, means that ewes in season may well be missed, while too many tups on the hill can also give rise to poor lambing results the following spring. The danger lies in the fact that some tups may not be able to take sole charge of a heft, but be forced to spend valuable time fighting off challengers, leaving the females' needs unsatisfied. In-bye shepherds – those whose flocks are always close to the buildings – usually put out an odd number of rams, as they call them, into a field of ewes. Then, in the event of battles breaking out between pairs of tups over the attraction of the moment, there is always one extra to do the necessary.

My stock is predominantly of the Scottish Blackface breed, a very hardy type of sheep and numerically the strongest in Britain today. The origins of the Blackface breed are shrouded in antiquity. They are first mentioned by Hector Boethius in 1460 who wrote that until the introduction of Cheviots, only the rough-woolled, black-faced sheep were to be found in the Vale of Esk in Dumfriesshire. In 1503, records assert that King James IV introduced 20,000 Blackfaces into the Ettrick Forest in Selkirkshire; unfortunately, no mention is made of where this enormous flock came from. Up until the 19th century, it was the custom for flockmasters to call their sheep by the name of the locality rather than by the breed. Thus, the Blackface was known simultaneously as the Linton, Forest, Tweeddale and Lammermuir, amongst others. Each area naturally believed that its flocks were the principal strain of the breed.

Blackface sheep did not appear in this part of Scotland before 1770. Previously the Highland grazings were stocked mainly by a small, old Celtic type of sheep, with a white face and soft Moorit (tan) wool, which can still occasionally be found on some of the offshore islands. There is a legend of an inebriate Perthshire publican who bought a few Blackface sheep which promptly escaped to the hill. Through sheer neglect, they were allowed to remain untended on the hill throughout the following winter. As it was the custom to house the Moorit sheep each night, the fact that these Blackfaces survived surprised many people and awakened interest in the breed. This story may only be a fable, but it is a fact that by 1767 Dumfriesshire flockmasters were renting many sheep-walks in Dunbartonshire and Perthshire. In 1770, there were around 1,000 Moorit-type sheep in this parish of Callander, and by 1790, the total had exploded past the 18,000 mark. Unfortunately, this increase in sheep numbers in the north and west of Scotland was accompanied by the enforced emigration of the human population – the iniquitous Highland Clearances had begun.

My four collies hold the tups tightly together just outside the hill gate. I use Mona and Gail to shed off two from the group, and start driving them in the direction of the Wee Hill. Bo, these days more usually called 'Gran' because of her 15 years, and Boot will watch over the others and stop any of them straying while I am away. Boot is a novice, still learning his job. He circles keenly round the tups, not allowing them the slightest chance to escape. Wise old Gran lies back a bit and watches, one eye on the tups, the other on me as I make my way towards the rising sun.

A little way ahead, a handful of sheep are grazing peacefully. Two or three look up at our approach. I call off the dogs and the two tups quickly come up, sniffing hopefully from one to another. Nothing doing here. Mona and Gail move them on.

A big ewe, tail-twitchingly in season, comes running down the hill towards us. Both tups oblige her in turn. No fighting; proper gentlemen. This gives me the ideal opportunity to split them up. I want to leave the younger tup at the bottom of the hill so that I can easily keep an eye on him. While he is busy with his paramour, I use the dogs quietly to work the other fellow, together with a few ewes, further up the hill. This tup ought to be able to cover the top ground of the Wee Hill.

Gran stirs herself, yawns, stretches and wags her tail at my return. Boot is still patiently 'wearing' the sheep in his charge as they pick at the grass shoots still to be found, sweet and succulent, under the twisted skeletons of fallen bracken. Mona separates out another pair of tups and Gail cuts in to help her take them straight up the hillside, en route for Meall Mór (Big Rounded Hill). The first of these I leave immediately above Spit Dubh (Black Spout), this morning a magnificent mare's-tail of silver, ice-sheathed water, highlighted against the backdrop of sheer black rock. The second tup has to keep climbing to come within sight of An t-Innean, the majestic Square Rocks which crown the summit of Glengyle.

A herd of red deer, suddenly alert to my presence, are startled into flight. Following their leader, they file away into the Braes of Balquhidder, white tail patches flashing in the bright sunshine as they go.

I descend by way of Allt na Bruiach (Steep Burn) which will bring me down a few hundred yards further up the glen. It is noticeable that the Scots were not very imaginative when it came to naming things. Indeed, the majority of Celtic names give either the simplest description of the place, or describe some prominent feature: big (*mór*), little (*beag*), black or dark (*dubh* or *dhu*), speckled or spotted (*breac*), crooked (*cam*), point (*stron*) as in Stronachlachar, Stonemason's point. Big hills (*meall mór*) and dark lochs (*loch dhu*) abound throughout Gaeldom. The Gael was also fond of giving the names of animals to many places associated with them. The Gaelic for a cow is '*bo*', as in *Baelach-nam-bo* – Pass of the Cattle – through which the old drove-road passed between Loch Katrine and Ben Venue; Loch Chon is Loch of the Dog; Brig O'Turk is Boar's Bridge. The list is apparently endless.

On the shoulder of Spit Dubh, 500 ft up, I have a clear view of the small group away down to my left. The tups browse whatever food they can find, still only yards from the hill gate. A couple of whistles pierce the crisp, clear air, riding down the wind. Gran rises to her feet and starts the tups moving towards me, along the well-worn sheep path at the back of the stone dyke. Several times Boot tries to pass the sheep and progress is interrupted. Each time I direct him back behind, the tups come on again. After yet another unscheduled stop, I decide to call him to heel and, once he has left the sheep and is safely on his way to me, I head for the bottom of the hill, leaving Gran to do the rest.

The red post-bus wends its way along the road to Glengyle with the morning post.

Boot is soon at my side, looking very pleased with himself. I make a fuss of him – reward is all important, especially during the early stages of training.

Near the foot of the hill is a small knoll (*Cnap beag*). By the time I reach it, Gran and the sheep are already in sight. The Steep Burn flows along beneath an overcoat of ice, and the tups carefully pick their way across. We move along between the top fence of my West Park and the last stand of birch trees in Glengyle. Long ago, the whole glen floor would have been well wooded with birch, oak, pine and alder. Man cleared the ground in the name of progress. Today, only the dark fingers of alder groves, pointing out the course of even the smallest flow of water, and a few isolated stands of birch and oak, remain in the glen. Lower down the strath, the wider part of the glen, modern plantations of fir trees have been established, with little regard for the eye or the delicate balance of nature.

Red Sky at Night

John Barrington

ISBN 0 946487 60 X PBK £7.99

This fascinating insight into a shepherd's life took *Red Sky at Night* to the top of the UK bestseller charts on first publication. Now with this new Luath edition a new generation of readers can discover the rhythms of the seasons, spend the night on the hill and learn the mysteries of how shepherds communicate with their dogs. From the reviews the book has received, it might be that the old chant, red sky at night, shepherd's delight, could be reworked: *Red Sky at Night*, reader's delight!

Mr Barrington is a great pleasure to read. One learns more things about the countryside from this account of one year than from a decade of The Archers.

THE DAILY TELEGRAPH

Powerful and evocative... a book which brings vividly to life the landscape, the wildlife, the farm animals and the people who inhabit John's vista. He makes it easy for the reader to fall in love with both his surrounds and his commune with nature.

THE SCOTTISH FIELD

Loch Lomond and the Trossachs: An A-Z of Loch Lomond and The Trossachs National Park and surrounding area

John Barrington

ISBN 1 905222 42 4 PBK £8.99

– How did the Devil form the Whangie?
– Where does the word 'blackmail' derive from?
– Which church minister was away with the fairies?
– How did Rob Roy defeat a troupe of Redcoats with an echo?
– Where can you see the Heavenly Dancers?

The answers to all these questions can be found in *Loch Lomond and The Trossachs*, John Barrington's follow up to the bestselling *Red Sky at Night*. Here, Barrington draws upon his wealth of knowledge and experience of life in Loch Lomond and surrounding Trossachs area to create a compelling historical, mythological and linguistic A to Z of the region.

This is an insider's recommendation of all you should see in this, Scotland's first national park, if you truly wish to uncover its beauty and find out all it has to offer. From the enchantments of the Aberfoyle landscape to the locality of the Zygaena moth, Barrington's love of his subject shines through as he explores the sites, characters and wildlife that make this area so attractive to tourists, historians and etymologists alike.

Luath Press Limited

committed to publishing well written books worth reading

LUATH PRESS takes its name from Robert Burns, whose little collie Luath (*Gael.*, swift or nimble) tripped up Jean Armour at a wedding and gave him the chance to speak to the woman who was to be his wife and the abiding love of his life. Burns called one of 'The Twa Dogs' Luath after Cuchullin's hunting dog in Ossian's *Fingal*. Luath Press was established in 1981 in the heart of Burns country, and is now based a few steps up the road from Burns' first lodgings on Edinburgh's Royal Mile.

Luath offers you distinctive writing with a hint of unexpected pleasures.

Most bookshops in the UK, the US, Canada, Australia, New Zealand and parts of Europe either carry our books in stock or can order them for you. To order direct from us, please send a £sterling cheque, postal order, international money order or your credit card details (number, address of cardholder and expiry date) to us at the address below. Please add post and packing as follows: UK – £1.00 per delivery address; overseas surface mail – £2.50 per delivery address; overseas airmail – £3.50 for the first book to each delivery address, plus £1.00 for each additional book by airmail to the same address. If your order is a gift, we will happily enclose your card or message at no extra charge.

Luath Press Limited
543/2 Castlehill
The Royal Mile
Edinburgh EH1 2ND
Scotland
Telephone: 0131 225 4326 (24 hours)
Fax: 0131 225 4324
email: sales@luath.co.uk
Website: www.luath.co.uk